"Give me a good reason to marry you."

"Sex," Garth answered Vicki bluntly. "I want you. And when you let yourself forget your inhibitions, you want me."

Vicki shook her head in mute denial, trying to forget those fleeting moments when every facet of her being had melted into a passionate longing for him. "No," she whispered. "That's the very worst of reasons to get married."

"Give me a better one!"

Beleaguered, she said the first thing that came into her head. "What about love? You've never mentioned the word."

She saw his tall frame shudder. As if he could not face her any longer, he turned his head toward the horizon, looking out over the ocean's cold gray wastes. Tonelessly he said, "I married once for love, Vicki. I won't do it again."

The Storms of Spring

by

SANDRA FIELD

Harlequin Books

TORONTO • LONDON • LOS ANGELES • AMSTERDAM
SYDNEY • HAMBURG • PARIS • STOCKHOLM • ATHENS • TOKYO

Original hardcover edition published in 1981
by Mills & Boon Limited

ISBN 0-373-02457-6

Harlequin edition published February 1982

CHAPTER ONE

THE storm had already started when Vicki went to the front door and looked out. Even though it was April, and winter should have been over, everything was coated with an inch-thick layer of glimmering ice: the shed, the clothes line, the trees. The wind had come up, and the branches clattered against each other, tiny shards of dislodged ice falling to the ground. The sky was a uniform dull grey-white, heavy with snow, and she felt the first qualms of apprehension; she could be marooned alone here for two or three days.

That was what she wanted, wasn't it? she thought fiercely. Solitude, peace and quiet. Well then, why was she complaining? Why this gathering sense of disquiet, this feeling of some impending disaster? It was, of course, nonsense . . . she was allowing her nerves to get the better of her.

Even so, she knew she would have welcomed the sight of Nils's sturdy figure tramping up the long driveway. But the frozen landscape remained empty of any other human, and the mournful keening of a herring gull, its plumage the colour of the sky, only added to her sense of loneliness. She went indoors and tried to work on her book, but the words would not flow; she picked up a sketch pad, but her pencil remained stubbornly still. Finally, in desperation, she stalked into the living room with a duster and mop and began to give the house a good cleaning, stopping only to put on a pot of stew for supper.

It must have been five o'clock when she finished. Going to the front door to shake out the hooked rugs, she was horrified by the deterioration in the weather; the world had become a whirling maelstrom of whiteness. She could no longer see the main road through the shifting clouds of snow, and the driveway had disappeared under an undulating white carpet. Drifts were already piling up against the side of the house, while around it the wind wailed like a creature in pain.

If she had had any half-formed notions about going to stay with Nils, they had disappeared—it would be madness to venture out in such weather. She was here to stay until the storm ended.

Vicki was about to turn back into the house when there was a lull in the wind and momentarily her vision cleared. Down by the road something moved, a dark patch against the snow. She frowned in concentration. But then the gale seized the snowflakes again, driving them like white sails through the sky, and the illusory movement was gone, vanished as though it had never been.

She waited, hugging the rolled-up rugs for warmth. Mocking her feeble eyesight, the snow danced and leaped in a maddened frenzy. It must have been her imagination, she thought uneasily. Earlier she had hoped to see Nils coming; now, out of an obscure need for company, she was conjuring up the sight of another person. That must be it.

She turned her back on the scene and went back into the house, closing the door firmly behind her. After replacing the mats, she washed her hands and added vegetables to the stew, intending to have a cup of tea while they were cooking. However, as if drawn by a magnet, she found herself at the front window, staring out into the storm. Into her mind's eye dropped the memory of that hint of movement, that dark patch at the edge of the road. Her brain working with absolute clarity, she knew it had been real. Something—or someone—was out there in the blizzard, hurt perhaps, or lost. And it was up to her to do something about it.

Her decision made, she moved with a quick precision, lighting the oil lamp and setting it in the front window where it would guide her home, finding a heavy-duty flashlight, lacing up her boots and pulling on her parka. She shoved an extra pair of mittens in her pocket and she was ready.

As she left the shelter of the front porch, the wind hit her like a blow, so that she staggered sideways, already blinded by the driving snow crystals. For a moment her heart failed her—she was mad to even attempt this. She beat a quick retreat into the house, and stood for a moment lost in thought. Then her eyes brightened. From the kitchen she took a big coil of thin, but very strong, nylon cord, and proceeded to tie one end to a fence post at the front of the house; she could pay out the rest of the line as she went, and that way she would be sure of finding her way back. She had heard stories of men getting lost between the house and the barn in a blizzard, and she had no desire to emulate them; it suddenly occurred to her that not even in the worst of the days of her marriage to Barry, or afterwards when she had been left alone again, had she ever contemplated suicide. Somehow she had struggled on from day to day, always with the need to survive. . . . And her life was better now, she thought stoutly, perhaps better than it had ever been except for those first golden weeks with him in Montreal. . . . Wincing away from memories she had never had the courage to examine, she brought her mind back to the concerns of the present.

The journey to the road seemed to go on for ever. All her senses were blunted by the storm—she could not see more than three feet in front of her, and to her ears came only the hiss of snowflakes as they hit the ground; all other sounds were muffled. Sometimes she sank knee-deep into the snow; sometimes the wind had scoured the ground bare so that her boots skidded on the ice and she would nearly fall. Praying that she was going in the right direction, she struggled on. It was only when she tumbled into the ditch that she knew she had reached the road. Getting to her feet, and brushing the snow from her parka, she looked around her.

'Halloo!' she yelled. 'Anyone there?'

The wind seized her voice and tossed it skyward. She turned on the flashlight, its yellow beam comfortingly normal in a world where nature seemed to have gone berserk, and holding the last coils of the rope, she began methodically tramping up and down the length of the ditch, peering through the snow, tripping over shrubs and boulders. No one . . . nothing. She was getting tired, she knew. Each time she fell to her knees, it was a little more difficult to get up, and she could hear her own breathing harsh in her throat. She had to leave herself enough strength to get back to the house. . . .

It was almost completely dark now. Dark and unbearably lonely. There was only herself and the writhing ghosts of snow, their voices the crying of the wind.

She fought back a primitive surge of terror. Trembling, shaken, she wanted only to return to the house: to warmth and light and all the comforts of reality. Scrambling out of the ditch, she looped the rope around her arm. She had done all she could, she thought wildly. Maybe, after all, she had been mistaken—all she had seen was a tree, or perhaps an animal.

Afterwards she never knew what it was that kept her from a headlong flight to the house. Some slight sound carried on the wind? Some primeval instinct that she was not alone? Her head swung to the left, towards a small copse of trees by the side of the road. She had not looked there—yet wouldn't it be a logical place for someone to take shelter? Training her flashlight ahead of her, she forged towards it through the drifts.

Her toe caught on something under the snow, and she pitched to the ground. At first she thought it was another rock, or a tree stump. But then she realised it was soft . . . and that it had moved.

Stifling an instinctive shriek of fear, she began brushing the snow away. A brown jacket, sleeves outflung, the hood pulled up. A small white face, wet dark lashes against waxen cheeks, and a tumble of soaked hair. She had found him . . . but was he even alive?

She turned the little boy's limp body face up, shining the light full on his face. There was an ugly bruise on his forehead and a scrape down one cheek. To her infinite relief she saw his eyelids flicker and open, revealing dazed grey eyes. Lowering the torch a little, she said quickly, 'It's all right—you're going to be okay.'

He did not seem to hear her. His eyes closed and his head fell back against her arm. Suddenly frightened, Vicki lowered her face to his and across her cheek felt the slow rhythm of his breathing. She shook him a little, but he had sunk back into unconsciousness. His hands were bare and cold to the touch; his jacket and jeans were wet through. She would have to hurry. . . .

If the journey to the road had seemed endless, the journey back became an unmitigated nightmare. The boy was only young, perhaps six or seven, but he was a dead weight in her arms and twice she fell heavily to the ground, bruising herself in an effort to shield him. Her limbs felt like lead weights and a stabbing pain pierced her chest with every step. Once she dropped the precious rope, and had to scramble for it in the snow, knowing now that two lives depended on it. Then, finally, the darkness was pierced by a dim glimmer of golden light: the lamp she had placed in the window. She had never seen anything more beautiful in her life, and she was almost weeping with relief as she pushed open the back door.

However, she could not rest yet. Laying the boy down on the couch in the kitchen, she stripped off his wet clothes, rubbed him down, and dressed him in an old pair of flannelette pyjamas. Putting a hot water bottle on his feet, she covered him warmly, and added more wood to the stove. Only then did she change from her own wet clothes.

He was stirring now, his thin body restless under the heaped-up blankets. He whimpered something under his breath and she bent to catch it, noting uneasily the hectic flush in his cheeks. 'Dad,' he muttered. 'Dad?' His eyes flew open. 'You've got to tell Dad where I am!'

'All right,' she said soothingly. 'But what's your name?'

For a moment the grey eyes were clear and rational. 'Stephen Travis,' he whispered. 'My dad's name is Garth. We live north of the mountain at Seal Cove.'

'But that's over a hundred miles away!' Vicki exclaimed. 'What are you doing down here?'

His eyes clouded and his lower lip quivered. 'It was my uncle—he took me away. You've got to tell my dad.' His fingers plucking at the covers, he began to cry. Vicki gathered him close, cradling the dark head to her breast until his sobs gradually lessened. She glanced down at the tear-streaked face and saw that he had fallen asleep.

Although she was very uncomfortable, her body twisted at an awkward angle, her arms cramped from holding him, she did not immediately release him. There was something about the feel of his frail body, the trusting way his head rested against her, that touched her to the heart, and she found herself blinking back tears. She had wanted to have children so much, but Barry had been adamantly against it, and as things had turned out, she supposed it was just as well. But now this unknown little boy had been catapulted into her life, and as she gently laid him back on the bed, his presence forced her to recognise that her present existence was a mockery of all her girlhood hopes. What she had wanted had been normal enough: a happy marriage and children. And both had been denied to her.

For a while she sat quietly watching him, pondering the little he had told her. The name Garth Travis meant nothing to her. Whoever he was, she could only presume that he did not know his son's whereabouts, and in such a storm he must be desperately worried; however, there was absolutely nothing that could be done until the weather cleared, for the nearest telephone was four miles away. She found herself wondering what Stephen had meant by the reference to his uncle; surely the boy had not been kidnapped? That sounded too bizarre. There must be some misunderstanding . . . but why had Stephen been wandering around in the dark with a bruise on his head, miles away from home? And where was the uncle now?

There would be no answer to these questions until tomorrow, she was sure, for by now the child was deeply asleep. She ate some of the stew, stoked up the furnace, and made up a bed in the living room, where she lay and read for half an hour before dimming the lamp. It was nice, she thought drowsily, to know there was someone else in the house in the midst of such a blizzard. . . .

Several times in the night she was awakened by Stephen's voice, usually calling for his father. Because of her broken rest, she slept later than usual in the morning and when she did wake up it was to find Stephen beside the bed, fully dressed, regarding her soberly.

'Who are you?' he asked. 'And how did I get here?'

The grey eyes were wary and still smudged with tiredness. She said quietly, 'My name is Vicki Peters. I saw you down by the road in the storm yesterday and brought you to the house. But I have no idea how you got there.'

'The man said he was my uncle Harold, and that he'd drive me home—I was waiting for the school bus, you see. But he didn't. He started going the wrong way. And when I told him, he told me to shut up.' The boy's voice trembled. 'He was driving too fast for me to jump out. And then it started to snow and he kept driving fast and I think there was an accident.'

Keeping her voice matter-of-fact, Vicki said, 'I see. Is that where you picked up the bruise on your head?'

He fingered it uncertainly. 'I guess so. I can't really remember. I know I was walking along the road trying to find someone and it was snowing so hard I couldn't see where I was going. I was lost. . . .'

Again that childish quiver of his lower lip that made her long to comfort him. Instead she said calmly, 'You did very well, because you reached the end of my driveway and that's how I found you.' She hesitated. 'So your father doesn't know where you are?'

'No. He'll be worried.'

He had not mentioned his mother, and somehow she knew better than to ask. Pulling on her housecoat, she got out of bed, wincing as her bare feet touched the cold floor. 'What's happening outside, Stephen?'

'It's snowing awfully hard.'

She looked out of the window and her heart sank.

Unrelieved whiteness as far as she could see—which was not very far, for snowflakes were falling from the sky with a kind of silent purposefulness that she knew only too well could go on for hours. She turned to face the boy, recognising the tension in the narrow shoulders and the almost adult air of anxiety. 'How old are you?' she asked with apparent irrelevance.

'Six and a half.'

At times he seemed older, at other times very much a child. 'Stephen,' she said steadily, knowing she had to be honest with him, 'I don't think we'll be able to get in touch with your father until it stops snowing——'

'But we've got to!'

'Listen a minute. Even if the telephones are working, which I rather doubt after all the freezing rain and high winds, the nearest one is four miles north of here. The snowploughs haven't been out yet—we'd never be able to make it.'

She could see him thinking this over. 'Oh,' was all he said, but he sounded so forlorn that she racked her brains for something more to say.

'The best thing we can do is stay around the house for now and keep warm, so you'll be in good shape when your father does get here. He wouldn't think either of us very smart if we went out in this kind of weather.'

'That's just the kind of thing he'd say.'

There was such a disgusted grimace on his face that she couldn't help laughing. 'Oh, dear, is it?' He was grinning too now, and their shared laughter seemed to forge a bond between them. Wanting to keep his mind off his concern about his father, Vicki said briskly, 'Let's go and light the kitchen stove and have breakfast. Then you can come to the barn with me to get the eggs.'

She managed to keep him occupied all morning, but after lunch she found him staring out of the window at the unending snow, his shoulders slumped. An easy companionship had already sprung up between them, and now he said, 'Vicki, what do you suppose happened to Uncle Harold?'

She had been hoping he would not ask. 'I don't know. I have a friend called Nils about a mile down the road— he's a fisherman. Maybe your uncle found his way there.'

'I wish I could remember—there must have been an accident. Perhaps he was hurt.' He shivered.

'Have you any idea why he'd try and take you away?' Even yet, she hated to use the word 'kidnap'.

'I think he hates my dad. Because of my mother, you see. So I expect that's why.'

This explanation only further increased Vicki's confusion, but all she said was, 'Well, there's no point in worrying about it, Stephen.'

'What'll we do if he comes here?' he blurted.

'Who? Your uncle?' The boy nodded wordlessly. 'I shouldn't think it's very likely, do you?'

'I think if he can, he will. He said he was going to make sure I'd never see my dad again.'

'Oh, Stephen. . . .' Even secondhand, she could sense the violence behind those words. She stooped down, bringing her face level with his. 'If your uncle does come, I promise you I won't let him take you anywhere—okay?'

'How will you stop him?'

She had no idea. 'I—I'd take an axe to him,' she said, trying to sound as if she meant it.

This bloodthirsty suggestion seemed to please Stephen. 'Let's put it out, so we'd be ready.'

Faintly horrified that he had taken her at face value, Vicki followed him out to the porch. 'There's a hatchet, too,' he said with considerable satisfaction. 'And what's this?'

'A splitting maul.'

'That should be enough.' He arranged the array of tools in the kitchen and then said prosaically, 'What are we going to have for supper? And you said you'd teach me how to play checkers.'

By dusk that evening it seemed as though the snow was clearing slightly, and for the first time in two days Vicki could see the jagged outlines of the trees down by the road. Surely the plough would be on the roads through the night so they'd be able to get to a telephone tomorrow, she thought hopefully; Stephen had not mentioned his father much throughout the day, but intuitively she knew how anxious the boy was to get in touch with him. Not for the first time she found herself wondering what kind of a man Garth Travis was—certainly there would appear to be a strong bond between father and son, a bond she couldn't help but envy. As she gazed out over the bleak landscape, she acknowledged to herself how much she would miss Stephen when he left, after only a day in his company. The house was going to seem very quiet without him. . . . She shivered and quickly drew the curtains, shutting out the darkness and the snow.

That evening the two of them played checkers again seated at the kitchen table, the stove murmuring and crackling cheerfully in the background, the battery-operated radio playing a Chopin recital by a celebrated pianist. It was a game for which Stephen had such an inborn flair that Vicki had to concentrate on every move, and they were so absorbed in their game that neither of them had any inkling that they were soon to be interrupted.

CHAPTER TWO

OUTSIDE the snow had almost stopped, only a few lazy crystals drifting earthward. High in the heavens stars glimmered, cold and remote, and a half moon was climbing in the sky, shedding a pale radiance over the black waters of the ocean and casting strange shadows on the smooth, unbroken snow. A preternatural stillness lay over everything; the trees drooped under their white burden and the air was sharp with frost.

Then, from the north, a man's figure appeared. He was wading through the thigh-deep snow on the road, his movements slow and laborious as though he was very tired. Across the glazed white fields he must have seen the soft glow of lamplight from the old farmhouse, for he halted for a minute, his body tense, his eyes fastened on the beacon of light with a desperate intensity. He turned towards it and began to push his way through the drifts; it was as though he had been injected with new energy, as though perhaps he sensed that his search was over.

The first that Vicki and Stephen knew of his approach was the sound of a fist banging on the back door. Stephen started so violently that two red checkers skidded across the board and rolled off the table. White-faced, he whispered, 'Do you think that's my uncle?'

His fear had spread to Vicki. Who else could it be? Nils always gave a special rap on the door, so it wasn't he . . . speaking very quietly, she said, 'Go into the living room, Stephen, and wait there—take the checkers with you. If it is your uncle, you're to hide in the cupboard. Don't come out until I tell you—okay?'

He nodded and tiptoed out of the room. Her heart thudding against her ribs, Vicki picked up the hatchet and went to the door. A second knock, more peremptory than the first. Taking a deep, steadying breath, she pulled it open, and light flooded out on to the porch.

The man blinked, temporarily blinded, then his eyes narrowed. 'What the hell are you planning to do with that?' he demanded, reaching over and removing the axe from her nerveless fingers. 'Whatever it was, I wouldn't advise it.'

She sagged aginst the doorpost, lightheaded with relief. The face looming above her was so like Stephen's that the stranger could be no one but Stephen's father. From the living room she heard running footsteps and a thin body hurtled past her and flung itself at the man. 'Dad—oh, Dad!' she heard Stephen cry, and then the boy's face was buried in the man's jacket.

Feeling like an intruder, Vicki saw the man's arms come hard around his son, saw the two dark heads come together, heard the deep voice say brokenly, 'Stephen— thank God! I thought you were dead!'

Such raw emotion was not for an outsider to witness. . . . Vicki turned away, her own vision blurred. So it was over, and father and son were together again. She walked through into the living room, where she gathered up the scattered checkers, automatically counting them to see if they were all there.

'Vicki! Where did you go?' Stephen's voice, shrill with excitement.

She moved to the doorway into the circle of light from the lamp on the kitchen table. The man looked at her intently, seeing a slim, straight figure in jeans and a heavy-knit sweater, with a mass of shiny dark hair framing a heart-shaped face and hazel eyes under dark-winged brows. She wore no make-up. Her features were perfect, but the curving mouth that should have been sensual was only deeply uncertain, and in the shadowed eyes was an incalculable sadness; her composure and control seemed too great for one so young.

As for Vicki, she saw father and son standing side by side, the man's arm around Stephen's shoulders. She had already been struck by the likeness between them. Now she saw differences. The thick hair, so dark as to be almost black, in the man was threaded with silver; his grey eyes were more guarded, less ready to trust. Features that in Stephen were still youthful and malleable, in Garth Travis had hardened and set. A firm chin, now stubbled with two days' growth of beard. An arrogant nose, high cheekbones, deep-set eyes, their sockets bruised and lined with exhaustion. He was not, she supposed, what one would call a classically handsome man: there was too much strength, too rugged and angular a cast to his features for that. He was, however, easily the most arresting man she had ever laid eyes on, so broad-shouldered and tall that her kitchen seemed to have shrunk.

Stephen broke the silence that for Vicki had gone on far too long. 'This is Vicki, Dad,' he said.

'The lady with the axe,' the man murmured.

She flushed. It might have seemed funny to him, but it had been less than amusing at the time. 'I'm Vicki Peters,' she said coolly. 'How do you do?'

'Garth Travis, Miss Peters.'

Her eyelids flickered. Without consciously making a decision, she said, 'It's Mrs Peters, actually.'

Stephen exclaimed, 'You didn't tell me you were married!'

'You didn't ask,' she answered, hoping her smile looked more natural than it felt.

'Where's your husband, then?' the little boy demanded, accusation in his voice.

'He's—away,' she said evasively.

'You don't wear a wedding ring,' Garth Travis interposed.

His voice was even, the steel-grey eyes emotionless. Why then did she know that he was suddenly violently angry? 'Neither do you,' she replied, after a lightning-swift glance at his hands.

'Stephen's mother's dead.'

'Oh.' She flushed. 'I'm sorry—I didn't know.'

He held out his hand. 'Well, Mrs Peters, it would seem I have a great deal to thank you for.'

Ignoring the outstretched hand, she disclaimed, 'I only

did what anyone else would have done.'

The anger was evident now, sparks struck from steel. 'Where I come from it's considered polite to shake hands.'

He had a genius for putting her in the wrong. Ungraciously she held out her right hand. His fingers, lean and well-shaped, closed around it. His palms were hard and calloused. Barry's hands had been whiter, softer, for Barry had been a man of the city. Barry . . . she could no more have prevented the shudder that ripped through her body than she could have stopped breathing. She snatched her hand away, rubbing it violently against her jeans.

'What's wrong?' Garth Travis demanded, his eyes boring into hers.

'Nothing.'

'Don't lie to me.'

Her chin tilted defiantly. 'Your hands are cold, that's all.'

'I don't believe you. But we'll let it ride for now,' he said with an undertone of menace.

'Your hands *are* cold, Dad,' Stephen piped; he had been trying to follow their conversation, his little face puzzled.

The man's features softened. 'Yeah, I guess they are. The temperature dropped about ten degrees in the past hour.'

He passed a hand across his face and Vicki suddenly realised that he was swaying on his feet. She pulled out a chair. 'Sit down before you fall down,' she said crisply. 'How long since you've eaten?'

It was a measure of his weariness that he obeyed her immediately, his shoulders slumped forward, his dark head bent. 'This morning, I guess,' he muttered. 'Or maybe it was last night.'

'I'll get you something to eat. Stephen, would you mind putting a bit more wood in the stove for me, please?' Moving with quick grace, Vicki soon had a meal prepared—steaming beef stew with thick chunks of home-made bread, and a piece of the chocolate cake she had made for Stephen earlier in the day; she had no difficulty in persuading the boy to have another piece now with a glass of milk, and as she placed the cake in front of him, she couldn't help smiling at his voracious appetite.

Garth Travis had not seen her smile before. It transformed her, ridding her face of that air of sadness, lightening the hazel eyes and tilting the soft mouth. But as she passed Garth the bread, her smile faded and visibly she retreated behind a polite mask. He made no comment. However, as she made the tea and served him more stew, his eyes followed her.

Vicki was aware of his scrutiny. Aware of it and frightened by it, although she would never have admitted that to anyone. She had already sensed that Stephen's arrival had disrupted the even tenor of her life, arousing all the old longings for a child of her own; his father, if she allowed him to, could disturb her even more. As he buttered a piece of bread, making some remark to his son, she studied him covertly, assessing the determined set of his chin and the ruthless mouth with its hint of sensuality. A strong man, and for her a dangerous man with his unsettling combination of startling good looks and formidable intelligence. And, she thought with uncomfortable honesty, something else: a masculinity, a sexual awareness, as much a part of him as the lithe movements and the proud bearing. Yes, he spelled danger. . . .

He had finished eating. 'Thanks, Mrs Peters——'

She hated the sound of that name, even though it gave her the protection she so badly needed. 'Please call me Vicki,' she interrupted. As she took away his plate, she once again saw him glancing at her ringless fingers.

'Very well,' he said smoothly. 'Thanks, Vicki—you're a good cook. I'm beginning to feel like life's worth living again. But it's bedtime for you, my boy.' Stephen's eyes had dropped almost shut. 'Where will he sleep, Vicki?'

'I closed off the upstairs for the winter. Maybe the two of you could sleep in my room—it's off the living room—and I'll sleep out here on the cot.' She felt a strong reluctance to put the stranger in her bed, but he was too tall for

the couch and she wanted to be in the kitchen so she
could keep the fires going. It was only for one night, after
all—what difference could it make?

Garth picked the boy up in his arms and followed her
into the bedroom. In one swift glance he took in the white
walls, the plain blue curtains and bedspread on the double
bed, the polished pine floor, smooth and cold. There were
no pictures or ornaments to indicate the personality of
the woman who slept there; it was as though she had
purposely erased all traces of herself.

'No photo of your husband?' Garth murmured as he
began to untie Stephen's boots; the boy had had no other
footwear with him.

'No,' she retorted. 'Should there be?'

'I would have thought it a little more normal. This,' he
looked disparagingly at the austere little room, 'looks like
a nun's cell.'

In the shadowed dimness of the room she was trapped
into honesty. 'It's too late for that,' she said bitterly.

Garth's back was towards her as he tucked Stephen
under the covers, so she missed the sudden intent look in
his eyes. All she saw was Stephen's arms flung around his
father's neck as the boy whispered, ''Night, Dad.'

'Goodnight, son.' Garth's voice was momentarily unsteady with a tenderness he made no attempt to hide.

''Night, Vicki.'

'Sleep well, Stephen,' she said, purposely removing any
emotion from her tone.

'I was beating you at checkers, wasn't I?'

The sleepy question unwittingly made her smile.
'Nonsense,' she said firmly.

'Oh yes, I was. Let's play again tomorrow, okay?'

'Okay,' she said, conscious of a little pang. Tomorrow
he would be gone. . . .

Garth followed her back into the kitchen. Over-
whelmingly aware of him, she busied herself at the sink,
wishing he too would go to bed and leave her alone.

'Do you miss your husband when he's away? Or doesn't
it happen very often?'

A knife dropped into the sink and her hands grew still. She had begun this deception, and now she would have to carry it through; it would be folly to abandon it with a man like Garth Travis. 'Of course I miss him,' she said evenly, rinsing off the plates.

'Turn around—I hate talking to someone's back.'

Slowly she did as she was told, bracing herself against the counter like an animal at bay. Across the room she met his gaze and the world narrowed to a pair of ocean-grey eyes, in whose depths she could drown. . . . Breathlessly she demanded, 'Why are you so interested in my husband?'

He parried her question with one of his own. 'What does he look like? Show me a picture of him.'

'I haven't got one,' she snapped, her fingers tightening unconsciously on the edge of the counter.

'You don't expect me to believe that?'

'I don't give a damn whether you do or not!' Driven to a kind of bitter honesty, she heard herself say, her voice raw with pain, 'I carry his image around with me—day and night. What do I need with photographs?'

There was a silence. Vicki felt a dull kind of wonderment, for she had seen him flinch at her words, and now there was a whiteness about his mouth, a baffled anguish in his eyes, that bewildered her. He straightened and came closer and she felt panic close her throat. 'What's the matter?' she whispered.

His eyes travelled over her, lingering on the long slender legs, the full breasts, the silken hair and fragile pointed face. 'Your husband is a lucky man—does he know that?'

Her voice was sharper than she intended. 'Why is he so lucky?'

His eyes widened in surprise. 'I would have thought it was obvious—you're the most beautiful woman I've ever seen.'

He could not have said anything more cruel, more calculated to hurt her. The tiny sound of her indrawn breath sounded shockingly loud. 'Don't!' she cried, her eyes pools of agony.

'Don't what, Vicki?'

'Don't say things like that when you know they're not true!'

He had grown very still, and had she known him better she would have been warned. 'I haven't said anything that's not the literal truth. You're a beautiful woman.'

'Stop!' she cried, almost incoherent with distress. 'Please stop——'

Visibly he fought for control. 'Okay. Just answer me one question, Vicki—who's done such a good job of convincing you you're not beautiful?'

It did not occur to her to lie. 'Barry, of course.'

'Who's Barry?'

'My—husband.'

'My God! Is the man blind?'

She gazed at Garth in silence. He was not doing this just to torment her or tease her, she thought dazedly. He must really think she was beautiful . . . but how could he? In the long months of their marriage, Barry had done his work all too well, and into her head floated the words he had used—plain, homely Vicki, the unsophisticated country girl, clumsy and awkward and graceless. . . . Knowing no better, lacking confidence to start with, she had believed him. Because he had made her nervous, she often had been clumsy and awkward in his presence. Because she had sensed his contempt, she had felt ugly. . . .

Bitter memories, memories she had tried to forget. Suddenly she buried her face in her hands.

'Look at me, Vicki.'

Slowly she obeyed him, her eyes shining with unshed tears. 'I——'

'I've upset you,' he said heavily. 'I'm sorry—I didn't mean to do that. I only want you to do one more thing, and then you'd better go to bed—it's getting late.' From the side of the cupboard behind her he unhooked the mirror that was hanging there. 'Come over here,' he said, taking it towards the lamp on the table.

She followed him obediently and as he held up the

mirror, she saw in it her own reflection.

'Remember when you and Stephen played checkers?'

She glanced up, the beginnings of a smile on her face. 'Yes.'

'You enjoyed it, didn't you?'

Her smile deepened and the big brown eyes softened. 'Yes, I did,' she admitted.

'Now look at yourself.'

In the mirror she saw a woman's mouth, gently curved, and lustrous brown eyes, warm with remembrance. She saw a shining fall of hair and delicately flushed cheeks.

'You're a beautiful woman, Vicki,' he said for the third time.

The colour spread in her cheeks, while pleasure and doubt warred in her features. 'Am I really?'

'Yes. I don't give a damn if you do love him—Barry is lying if he tells you you're not beautiful. I want you to remember that.'

'I—I'll try.' Almost then she told him the truth, but some obscure instinct of caution held her back. 'I don't understand why you did this,' she said, 'but thank you.'

There was an ugly twist to his mouth. 'I don't know why, either,' he said roughly. 'I must be crazy.'

His sudden change of mood frightened her and she retreated into practicalities. 'I'm going to put some wood in the furnace—do you have everything you need?'

He gave a short, humourless laugh. 'Far from it,' he said cryptically.

'I——' She was too tired to take up the challenge implicit in his words. 'Goodnight, Garth.'

'Goodnight.'

Quickly she attended to the fires and then turned out the lamp, undressing in the dark. She was desperately weary, for Garth had made her remember things she did not want to remember, and now it was hard to force them back into obscurity. For a long time she lay wide-eyed, staring up into the darkness.

She woke up because she was cold. The kitchen fire had gone out and the furnace must need more wood, she knew. Plucking up her courage to face the chilly air, she thrust her feet into slippers and padded down to the basement, trying to be as quiet as she could. When she came back upstairs, carrying the lamp with her, the kitchen was already warmer, for the fire was spitting and crackling in the stove and Garth was adjusting the dampers.

'Doesn't take long to cool off, does it?' he said impersonally.

'No.' She smiled faintly. 'My feet are like ice.'

'How much milk have you got? Enough for hot chocolate?'

'Oh yes, there's lots.' She put the lamp on the checkered tablecloth. When she had moved into the house last autumn she had taken the trouble to strip the old paint from the woodwork and panelling in the kitchen, and now the wood shone softly with its natural patina. An inexpensive but attractive floral wallpaper and bright curtains gave the room a cosiness and charm of which she was justifiably proud. That the kitchen reflected quite a different woman than did the bedroom had never occurred to her.

She put two mugs on the table and began mixing the cocoa and sugar in each, her face intent on the task.

'You really *are* married, are you, Vicki?'

She gave a guilty start. 'I wish you'd drop the subject of my husband and my marriage.'

'I asked you a question.'

'Yes, I'm married!' she snapped. 'I said I was, didn't I?'

He looked at her fixedly. Before going to bed she had pulled back her hair with a ribbon; she was wearing a long white chemise, with a high embroidered collar and frilled sleeves that fell over her wrists; it disguised her figure completely, drawing attention both to her youth and fragility, and to a certain innocence of demeanour of which she was quite unaware.

'I can't believe you've ever been touched by a man,' Garth said bluntly. 'You look as pure as the driven snow in that outfit.'

'What an appropriate simile under the circumstances,' she said sweetly.

'Don't be a bitch, Vicki. It doesn't suit you.' He paused. 'To be frank, I'd be willing to bet that you're a virgin.'

She paled. 'Don't be ridiculous!' The other words that Barry had used came flooding into her mind. Words like cold and frigid. Hurtful words. She fought them back, her face set, knowing that Garth Travis was watching her and that he must never know the truth. 'I'd be willing to make a bet, too, but I'd win mine,' she said coldly. 'I'd bet you're easily the rudest and most insufferable man I've ever met in my life.' Her voice gathered fire. 'I don't know what gives you the right to ask all these questions!'

'Don't you, my dear?' he said grimly. 'I'm not at all sure I'm going to enlighten you, so that seems to be that, doesn't it?' Restlessly he got up from the table, the light playing on his tautly muscled chest, dark with tangled hair; he was wearing only a pair of jeans. He moved with an animal-like grace that, in spite of herself, fascinated her in so big a man; there was not a single wasted movement.

Coming back from the stove, he poured the hot milk into the mugs and sat down across from her. To her relief he had decided upon a change of subject. 'There's something I want to ask you, and now's as good a time as any, with Stephen asleep. He told me his uncle took him away. Did he tell you much of what happened—with Harold, I mean?'

That question she could answer, and imperceptibly she relaxed in her chair. 'No, not really. He said his uncle met him on the way from school, took him in the van on the pretext of going to your house, and then proceeded to drive south. When Stephen tried to get out, Harold wouldn't let him. Stephen couldn't even remember whether there'd been an accident—although I think there must have been, don't you? He had an awful bruise on his forehead.'

'How did you find him?'

'I saw him from the window—he was in the grove of trees by the road.'

'You saw him in the midst of a blizzard?' By persistent questioning, Garth extracted the story from her of the long struggle through the snow, of her near-abandonment of the search, and of her final discovery of the boy under the snow.

'He was unconscious . . . so you had to carry him?'

'Well, yes,' she said uncomfortably. 'It's a good thing he wasn't much bigger!'

'I owe you a debt of gratitude I can never repay, Vicki,' Garth said with complete seriousness. 'You saved his life— he'd have frozen to death if you hadn't brought him to the house.'

She fiddled with her mug and said awkwardly, 'Well, I suppose so. But now it's your turn for explanations. How did *you* get here?'

He grinned ruefully, the muscles rippling under his skin as he leaned back in the chair. 'With great difficulty,' he said. 'The day that Stephen disappeared, I couldn't do a thing. The roads were totally impassable and the visibility was zero.' His face hardened in remembrance. 'I think that was the longest day of my life—I've never felt so utterly helpless. But the next day the weather had improved enough that I could borrow a neighbour's skidoo. One of Stephen's friends had seen Stephen get in the van, and knew it was headed south. So I headed south too—stopping at every second or third house to ask if anyone had seen them. The telephones are out all along the shore, so there was no way I could call the police. The last person to have seen them was about twenty miles from here—after that, nothing.'

Vicki could imagine all too well the things he was not saying—the discouragement of being turned away without news time and again, the ever-gathering fear for his son. Just to have kept the skidoo on the road for all that distance, battling against the wind and the cold, was an accomplishment in itself. She felt an unwilling respect for this man, whose love for his son had driven him into danger and darkness.

'The skidoo broke down about a mile from here,' Garth

continued. 'I had the choice of going back three miles or pushing on and hoping I'd come to a house. Fortunately I came to yours.' His eyebrow quirked. 'And was greeted with an axe!'

She said crossly, 'We were afraid you might be Harold—Stephen's really afraid of him, you know.'

'Harold is nearly six feet tall and weighs over two hundred pounds.'

'Well, I can't help that! I wasn't just going to stand by meekly and let him take Stephen away again.'

'You're quite a woman,' Garth said softly. 'I'm sure I could pick you up with one hand, and yet you weren't afraid to tackle a kidnapper with an axe——'

Embarrassed, she said lightly, 'I didn't say I wasn't afraid!' He could pick her up, she knew, and felt a flutter of panic at the thought. Taking a sip of cocoa, she said, 'Maybe it's none of my business—but why would Stephen's own uncle try to kidnap him?'

'You have a perfect right to ask, after everything you've done for us.' He traced a pattern on the tablecloth with his fingernail, his face suddenly harsh and forbidding. 'Harold, as far as I know, has been in the Middle East for the past three years—he's a geologist, works with one of the big oil companies. He was always very close to my late wife—the protective older brother—they corresponded regularly and I'm sure he felt I'd treated her very badly over the years. Perhaps out there in the desert, with not much else to think about, he brooded about it all too much. When Corinne was killed just over a year ago, I had a letter from him, full of threats of how he was going to get even with me—and one way to hurt me is through Stephen, of course.'

Unconsciously Vicki moved back in her chair, appalled by the brief little story, a story which raised more questions than it answered. A brother journeying across half the world from the scorching deserts of the East to this land of ice and snow, to avenge his dead sister. How had she died? What had been done to her that she had appealed to him for help? Through new eyes she saw the ruthless line of Garth's jaw, the gash of his mouth, the power implicit in those lean fingers. . . .

'Don't look at me like that!' he said harshly. 'I didn't murder her, you know.'

She shivered. She had always had too vivid an imagination, and now it was only too easy to put herself in the dead Corinne's shoes, and to imagine herself at the mercy of Garth Travis . . . she could feel those hands slide to her throat, feel the powerful body pinioning her to the wall.

'I—I didn't say you did,' she murmured faintly. 'But Garth, if you're right about Harold—what do you suppose has happened to him?'

'I don't know, Vicki. We'll just have to hope that tomorrow will bring some answers.'

Tomorrow. . . . 'I'm going back to bed,' she said, striving for a normal voice, 'or I won't be good for anything tomorrow.'

As she stood up, so too did he. But instead of leaving the room, he came around the table towards her. Trying to ignore him, she picked up the mugs and rinsed them out in the sink. The hairs on the back of her neck prickled and she knew he was right behind her.

'Vicki?'

There was no reason to be afraid, no reason at all. She turned to face him. 'Yes?'

He reached up a hand and stroked the heavy fall of hair back from her face, his fingers brushing her skin. Taut as a strung bow, she suffered his touch, her eyes huge in a face of deathly pallor. 'Thank you for giving me back my son, Vicki,' he said, his face so close to hers that she could see tiny dark flecks in the grey of his irises. Then his hands fell to her shoulders and she knew he was going to kiss her. . . .

Panic exploded within her. She pushed him away with all her strength, her voice high-pitched with terror. 'Don't! Don't touch me!'

He made no effort to bridge the gap between them. His eyes were watchful on her stricken face, on the frantic pulse at the base of her throat. 'You're over-reacting. I wasn't going to rape you. I only wanted to express my gratitude to you.'

Her breathing still raggged, she reiterated, 'I hate to be touched.'

'That must be inconvenient for your husband.'

She flinched, trying to gather her scattered wits. 'I should have said I hate being touched by anyone else, then.'

'I see. Well, he certainly doesn't have to worry about you being unfaithful to him, does he, if you react like that every time someone comes near you.'

'I shall never be unfaithful to him.'

There was the ring of absolute truth in the quietly spoken words. In a gesture of overwhelming frustration the man suddenly hit the table with his clenched fist.

The sound was like a whipcrack in the night and Vicki quivered as though it was she who had been struck. 'Why did you do that?'

'The gods must be laughing,' he said savagely. 'Let me tell you something, Vicki—sweet, innocent Vicki, who won't even let me touch you. For the first time in God knows how long I've met a woman who could mean something to me. A woman of beauty and great courage. A woman of untapped passions—I would swear to that. Capable of loving with an intensity she's never realised.'

He halted just as abruptly as he had begun, fighting for breath. Vicki waited, trembling in every limb. Finally he looked up, his grey eyes piercing her very soul. 'That woman is you, Vicki. And by one of those ironies of fate, you're married.'

As though he had to put a physical distance between them, he strode over to the door and then faced her again, his big body filling the doorway. 'And because you're you,' he went on more quietly, 'that marriage is a lifelong commitment. You'll never leave him, or be unfaithful to him. Will you?'

She shook her head, each word like a blow. Somehow she had to end this, she who had started it with a simple

enough deception. She had been right to deceive him,
she knew that now—if Garth knew her to be free, what
might he not have done? She stifled the tiny flow of wonderment deep within her that this powerful, arrogant
stranger had found her attractive and desirable, and said
coldly, 'Tomorrow you'll be gone. You'll forget me soon
enough.'

'And what if I don't?'

She quailed inwardly at the menace implicit in his
question. 'You have no choice,' she said, fighting for
control.

'I can't believe that!'

'You must.'

He straightened to his full height, the deep-set eyes
shadowed. 'We'll see about that, Vicki Peters. Yes, I'll
leave tomorrow. But I don't promise to stay out of your
life. You were meant for me, I know you were.'

'You're wrong!' she gasped, knowing she was at the
end of her strength, battered almost to her knees by the
sheer force of his will. If he ever found out the truth, she
would be helpless against him. . . . 'Please go now, and
leave me alone.'

'Very well—but don't think this is the end, will you?'

She muttered an inaudible reply, hearing his footsteps
cross the living room floor and then the creak of the bedroom door. Her knees gave way and she sank down on
the cot, staring blankly at the opposite wall. Garth Travis
spelled danger . . . danger to the safe little world she had
rebuilt from the ruins of the old one. Nothing must destroy
that safety, nothing. Tomorrow he would be gone and she
could forget about him, she thought, huddling under the
covers. Finally, soothed by the gentle hum of the fire, she
fell asleep.

CHAPTER THREE

WHEN she awoke, burrowed in the warm cocoon of blankets, it was morning and the clear spring sunlight was pouring in the window. She lay still. It was as though the sun had permeated her body with its promise of summer to come, for of all of yesterday's events she found herself remembering Garth's words in the middle of the night—he had called her a woman of beauty and courage, a passionate woman to whom he was strongly attracted . . . as if he was standing in front of her, she could see the rangy, muscular body, the harshly carved face with its moody grey eyes and thatch of dark hair; and under the sun's rays, wonderment, like a flower, opened its petals within her. On sudden impulse she got out of bed and took the tiny mirror off the wall. Standing full in the light, she held it up and gravely regarded herself, her hazel eyes full of questions.

She did not hear the pad of bare feet approaching the kitchen. It was a flicker of movement in the doorway that caught her eye; looking up she saw Garth watching her soberly. For a moment she remained transfixed, a slim white-clad figure outlined in gold. Then she blushed and thrust the mirror back on to its hook. 'You're up early,' she said ungraciously.

'I heard the snowplough a while ago, so I decided to get up.'

She pulled back the curtains and sure enough there were banked-up heaps of snow all along the road. So there would be nothing to keep him here any longer. . . .

'The nearest police detachment is ten miles south of here, isn't it? I guess I'll have to report that Harold's missing—do you mind looking after Stephen for me while I do that? I don't particularly want him involved any more than is necessary.'

'Of course you don't,' she agreed. 'And of course I'll stay with him.'

'Thanks.'

For a minute she thought he was going to say something else, but then the moment passed, leaving her with a curious sense of disappointment. She murmured, 'I'd better get dressed, then, and get you some breakfast.'

'Okay—I'll look after the fires.'

By the time she was dressed and had the porridge bubbling on the stove, Stephen had joined them in the kitchen, and so they all sat down together to eat, putting brown sugar and thick creamy milk on the steaming bowls of cereal. The sharing of the chores with Garth earlier, and now the sharing of a meal—simple enough things, yet they gave Vicki an inkling of a kind of companionship that was new to her. This was what a real family would be like, she thought painfully, as she took the toast out of the warming oven and put it on the table. She remembered the aunt and uncle with whom she had grown up—a stern-faced couple, as bleak and unyielding as the rocky acres they had farmed in northern New Brunswick. They had taken her out of charity, and over the long months and years had never ceased to remind her of that. There had been precious little laughter in that house, she thought, hearing Garth chuckle at some quip of Stephen's.

'Oh, look, there's someone coming, Vicki,' Stephen piped.

She dragged herself back to the present, unaware of how vividly her thoughts had been reflected in her face or how closely Garth had been watching her, and glanced out of the window. A man on snowshoes, carrying a backpack, was coming towards the house.

'It's Nils,' she said, pleasure colouring her voice.

'Who's Nils?' Garth rapped.

Taken aback by his peremptory tone, she said defensively, 'A friend of mine from down the road. He has a Jersey cow and keeps me supplied with milk. Excuse me a minute.'

She got up from the table and went to the back door,

pulling on her parka and boots and tramping down the snow around the doorway. When Nils came round the corner, she cut across his greetings unceremoniously. 'Nils, I have visitors,' she said quietly. 'I'll explain later—but if they ask, my husband still lives with me. He's just away right now, okay?'

Although obviously puzzled, he said goodnaturedly, 'Okay. Where is he? Your husband, I mean.'

'Shh—they'll hear you! *I* don't know—on an oil tanker, or something. Let's hope it won't even come up.'

He unlaced the snowshoes and knocked the snow off his knee-high moccasins. He was only an inch or so taller than she, a stockily built young man with the silver-blond hair and far-seeing blue eyes of his Scandinavian ancestors. Although it was April, and the end of a long and bitter winter, his skin was weathered and against it his beard was startlingly fair. 'There's nothing wrong, is there?'

'No. But you know me—I want to stay uninvolved. And this man—well, you'll see him. I just thought it was better to pretend that I was still married.'

'I see. Got the coffee on?'

'Sure—come on in. Is that fresh milk?'

'Yeah—and a bottle of cream too.'

Vicki led Nils into the kitchen. Garth got to his feet, towering over the younger man. Shrewd blue eyes met cool grey ones as Vicki made the introductions and poured some more coffee. Then they were all seated again.

'Oh, I nearly forgot,' said Nils, reaching into his backpack. 'I brought you a present, Vic. I made it during the storm.' He held out a newspaper-wrapped object.

'How nice of you!' she said warmly, peeling off the paper, and hoping it would be one of his wood carvings. She fell silent, for in her hands was one of his carvings, but this one was of herself. She was standing on a small knoll, a hand to her eyes as she gazed into the distance; the wind had moulded her clothes to the slim lines of her figure and had tossed her hair out behind her. Somehow he had drawn from the inanimate wood a sense of poised expectancy and an undoubted gallantry. She could not help being reminded of Garth's words to her, the words she had woken up remembering.

'Thank you, Nils,' she said softly, a sparkle of tears in her eyes. 'It's beautiful.'

He flushed a dull brick red. 'You're welcome.'

'It's beautiful indeed,' said Garth, an odd note in his voice; Vicki could see him reassessing the young fisherman with his work-roughened hands and wind-burned face. 'Do you do much of that sort of thing, Nils?'

'All winter. Along with building lobster traps and the occasional dory,' Nils said gruffly. 'Then I fish all summer.'

'Have you ever had any formal training?'

'I spent two years in Toronto and took a course there.' Nils grinned crookedly. 'The usual story—country boy heads for the big city to make his fortune. Only it didn't turn out that way. I hated it. Still, it got the travel bug out of my system, so I could come back here to Cape Breton where I belong.'

'Some time I'd like to see the rest of your carvings.'

'Sure. You from around here?'

Vicki and Stephen cleared away the dishes as Garth explained his presence and in the end the two men had arranged to go together to find transport for the trip to the police; a rapport seemed to have sprung up between them despite a certain wariness on both sides.

Garth was gone until mid-afternoon. During his absence Stephen and Vicki had done the chores and then had built a huge snowman in front of the house, decorating its face with rocks and making hair out of straw. They spent the afternoon tobogganing down the slope behind the house, and somehow this turned into a snowball fight. As Garth trudged up to the house, he heard the sounds of shouting coming from the woods and went to investigate. It looked as though Vicki was winning, for she had Stephen trapped in a culvert and was showering him with loose snow. An unholy light of mischief in his eye, Garth slid behind a tree and made a snowball, firing it

with deadly accuracy. It caught the girl on the shoulder
and, laughing, she whirled to face the new challenge.

With Stephen and Garth ganging up on her, Vicki
didn't have a chance. Within a few minutes she was
pinned against a rock face as her two opponents bombar-
ded her. 'Stop!' she shrieked. But Stephen had crept up
on her to thrust a handful of snow down her neck. Trying
to escape him, she whirled and ran right into Garth, his
solid body knocking the breath from her lungs.

Time was suspended . . . her face vivid with life, her
tawny eyes dancing, she gazed wordlessly up into the face
so close to hers. He was smiling at her, a strange tenderness
in the strongly carved features; she could feel the steel
strength of his arms, and a weakness invaded her limbs.
He was so big, looming over her. So tough and undeniably
male. He made her feel small and fragile—and somehow
cared for. With a tiny shock of discovery she knew he
made her feel like a woman. Forgetting that she hated to
be touched and held, and ignoring the danger signals that
he always aroused, she felt herself drowning in the grey
depths of his eyes and unconsciously her body relaxed in
his grip, her hair falling across his shoulder.

'Put her down, Dad!' Stephen cried. 'Put her in the
snowbank!'

'Really, Stephen,' Garth drawled, his eyes never leaving the girl's bemused face, 'as if I'd do a thing like that!'

'Do it, Dad, do it!'

Garth grinned down at Vicki, 'Shall I?'

She blinked, trying to free herself from those hypnotic
grey eyes. 'No,' she gasped, scarcely knowing what she
was saying. 'No, don't!'

'The lady says no, Steve,' Garth said, regretfully releasing her. 'Still, I think it's pretty obvious we won, don't
you?'

Still trying to get her breath back and feeling as though
something momentous had happened, Vicki said, 'Two
against one—I should hope you did win! You can't trust
men to play fair.' She had meant that last as a joke, but
the words came out with a bitter ring to them and she

was suddenly appalled to recollect how close she had felt
to Garth just a few moments ago. She was mad to let
down her defences even for an instant. She had done that
once before, and look what had happened. . . .

'Don't generalise,' Garth snapped. 'You can't trust *some*
men—just as you can't trust some women. On the other
hand, there are certain people you could trust with your
life.'

'I'll never do that again,' she said clearly.

'Then yours will be the loss,' was the grim reply.

'What do you mean?' she faltered.

'Simply if you cut yourself off from people, then you'll
find yourself alone—and only half alive. Sure there are
risks in trusting people, in being intimate—but there are
also great rewards.'

'Not for me,' she whispered, looking past him into the
sombre depths of the forest. He took a step towards her,
then halted in frustration.

Stephen had been listening uncomprehendingly. 'Dad,
my feet are cold,' he complained.

'Okay—we'd better go in.'

In a silence that was all the more noticeable because of
their previous exuberance, they trailed back to the house.
As Garth was unlacing Stephen's boots in the back porch,
Vicki heard him say, 'I went to see the police this afternoon, Stephen. There *was* an accident the other day—
they found your uncle's van in a ditch not far from here.
He was dead—he'd been killed right away. So even if
we'd known where he was, we wouldn't have been able to
do anything.'

'Oh,' said Stephen in a small voice. 'He was a bad
man, wasn't he, Dad?'

'It was certainly bad of him to take you away from
me.'

'Now I won't have to worry about him doing it again.'

'Were you worrying about that?' his father asked.

'Oh yes. I was scared of him.'

'Well, it's over now and best forgotten,' said Garth.

Admiring the straightforward way Garth had told his

son the truth about the accident, Vicki said casually, 'Roast chicken for supper—how does that sound? It should be ready in about an hour.'

While they were eating, Garth said to Stephen, 'I made arrangements for a car to pick us up about seven this evening to take us home.'

A forkful of potato halfway up to his mouth, Stephen wailed, 'We're going home tonight?'

'Yes, we have to. You have school tomorrow.'

'But I want to stay here another day!'

Impatiently Garth said, 'I'm sorry, you can't.'

'Can Vicki come with us, then?'

There was a perceptible pause. 'Certainly she may, if she wants to,' Garth said finally.

'You'll come, won't you, Vicki?' Anxious grey eyes pleaded with her to say yes. So he too had felt a closeness between them, a bond . . . knowing she was going to disappoint him, she felt a pang of guilt. 'I can't, Stephen.'

'Why not?'

'This is my home—I live here. I can't just pick up and leave——'

'It's only for a visit!'

'Who would feed the chickens? And keep the furnace going?'

His bottom lip was trembling. 'But I want you to come,' he said unanswerably.

And part of her wanted to go, for by some mysterious alchemy Stephen had already become the son she had never had, and the tears that hung on his lashes cut her to the quick. She must end this, she thought. There was no place in her life for a small boy, or for his handsome, disturbing father. 'I'm sorry, Stephen,' she said quietly, 'but it's impossible.'

He must have recognised the finality in her voice. The tears spilled over and he pushed his plate away. 'I don't want any more,' he cried, getting up from the table and running into the bedroom. The door slammed shut behind him.

'There's no excuse for that kind of behaviour,' Garth

said heavily, 'and I'll speak to him about it later. But couldn't you have at least promised to visit him in a few days, if not right away?'

Her face mirrored her conflicting emotions: guilt and unhappiness, overlaid by a stubborn determination not to give in. 'I don't make promises that I know I won't keep. Besides, both of you seem to forget I'm married.'

'So you're going to play it safe, Vicki, are you?' he grated. 'And to hell with Stephen's feelings.'

She quailed before the contempt in his face. 'It's not like that!' she burst out. 'You don't understand.'

'I could, if only you'd explain.'

He was like a battering ram, destroying all her defences. Looking anywhere but at him, her glance fell on the kitchen clock: six o'clock. Only one more hour and they would be gone. She scarcely knew any longer whether she wanted them to go or not. . . .

Garth suddenly changed tactics. 'Look, Vicki,' he said more quietly, 'you know how deeply I'm indebted to you because of Stephen—let me do something for you in return.'

Puzzled, she murmured, 'There's no need for that.'

Disregarding her, he plunged on. 'There's something badly wrong in your life, isn't there? I don't know what it is—although I'd guess it concerns your husband. Am I right?'

She gazed at him dumbly, pinned by the merciless grey eyes. He *was* right, of course, but she couldn't tell him that.

'You're unhappy with him, aren't you,' he said, more as a statement than a question. 'Is he cruel to you?'

She got a grip on herself. 'No,' she said, her voice far too loud.

'You can't tell me you're happy with him! Why don't you leave him, Vicki? Now—before you get tied down with children.' As she flinched, he went on roughly, 'Look at you! You're like a ghost. Do you realise this afternoon was the first time I'd heard you laugh? You're only a young woman—are you going to live the rest of your life in limbo like this? No man is worth that, Vicki.'

'Perhaps I'm in love with him.'

'If you think you're in love with him, you don't know the meaning of the word love.'

Her only defence was anger. 'I've already told you you have no right to talk to me like this!'

'Yes, I do—because I want you, Vicki, that hasn't changed.'

'Want me—what for?' she cried.

'I want to make you happy. I want to make you laugh again. Is there anything wrong with that?'

'Yes, there is—because I'm married,' she said steadily.

'Married to a man who leaves you alone in an old house miles from anywhere. A place with no telephone and no electricity——'

'I can manage very well on my own!'

'Sure you can—but what if you had an accident? What if you cut yourself splitting wood? What if you tripped and fell down the basement stairs? Who'd look after you then?'

Throughout the winter Vicki knew Nils had kept a fairly close eye on her, but she had always managed to shrug off her concern and go her own way. With Garth it was different. A tiny pocket of warmth circled around her heart.

With uncanny perception Garth said, 'Nils, I should imagine, must worry about you sometimes. What about your husband—does he? Does anyone else?'

She looked back into the past, journeying a long way from the cheerful little kitchen with its crackling fire. Her parents had died before she could remember them. Her aunt and uncle had seen her as a poor substitute for the son they had never had and had used her accordingly: they had never worried about either her physical well-being or her emotional state. As for Barry ... he had worried about her money, she thought cynically. Until he had gone through it all. And he had worried about her looks, wanting her to be a carbon copy of his friends' overdressed wives with their expensive clothes and their perfumes and their malicious tongues ... he had worried about all the wrong things.

'You don't have to answer me,' Garth said. 'I can tell by your face. I've only got one more question, Vicki, and I think I know the answer already. Do you like going to bed with your husband?'

Scarlet colour washed over her face. Covering her ears with her hands, she stammered, 'I don't want to hear any more!'

He grabbed her wrists and pulled her hands down, holding them imprisoned, and his voice beat at her ears. 'Do his kisses bring you to life? Do you ache to feel his hands on your body?' He gave a ugly laugh. 'You don't even know what I'm talking about, do you?'

She found herself staring at the hands encircling her wrists. His fingers were long and lean and shapely; in contrast, her own hands looked small, fragile, very feminine. The warmth of his palms seemed to scorch her skin. What would it feel like if one of those hands were to leave her wrist and stroke the soft flesh of her arm? she wondered. Would the warmth spread until her whole body was suffused with it?

Thoughts new to her. Alien to the kind of person she thought she was . . . for no reason that she could understand, tears trembled on her lashes. She wouldn't cry, she thought wildly—that would be the final humiliation. With all her strength she jerked her wrists free and pushed back her chair. 'It's time you got ready to leave,' she said, her voice so thin as to be scarcely recognisable. 'And don't come back.'

Garth stood up. 'It's hard to understand how you can be so brave in some ways and so cowardly in others. Maybe you're right—I'm crazy to even want to see you again. I'm better off leaving you as you are—half alive, locked in a marriage that's destroying you. Frozen, like the ground under the snow. Maybe there won't ever be a spring for you, Vicki. . . .'

'I don't know what you're talking about,' she whispered.

'Yes, you do.' He rubbed his forehead with his fingers,

his grey eyes baffled and helpless. 'I guess this is good-bye, then. You can forget what I said about wanting you for myself—because you were right, it's impossible.'

This was what she had wanted, wasn't it? Garth Travis out of her life. Why then did she feel anguish knife-sharp twisting within her?

'I just wish to God I'd never met you,' he muttered almost inaudibly.

Her nerves stretched to the breaking point, Vicki was conscious of an absurd desire to reach up her hand and smooth the lines from his forehead. She clenched her fingers at her side.

'Promise me one thing.' His voice was dull, almost life-less.

'Yes.'

'If you ever need a place to go, or anyone to help you—at any time, day or night—will you get in touch with me?'

'Yes, Garth, I will,' she said, knowing as she spoke that she never would.

Slowly he walked around the table towards her until they were only a few inches apart. She stood her ground, her heart banging against her ribs so loudly she was sure he must hear it. When he spoke she had to strain to hear him. 'I wish I could understand why it had to happen this way,' he said. 'Goodbye, Vicki.' And then he was walking away from her towards the bedroom to get Stephen.

Five minutes later they were gone. From the window she watched the two figures walk down the track that Nils had made in the snow, towards the headlights waiting at the side of the road. There had been a last-minute flurry of goodbyes. Stephen had hugged her fiercely, his face still streaked with tear-marks, and the feel of his thin little body in her arms had almost weakened her resolve. But then Garth had said gruffly, 'Come on, son, time to go,' and the moment had passed. Garth had not touched her again, nor even looked at her directly; his goodbye could have been to any chance-met stranger.

The headlights started to move and then the car was out of sight. They were gone. . . .

The house seemed suddenly very quiet. The wood snapped in the stove. The lamps hummed faintly. Melting snow dripped from the eaves. That was all. No footsteps or voices. No chatter around the table or laughter outside in the snow. She was alone again, alone as she had wanted to be.

The next two weeks passed slowly. As if to make amends for the blizzard, the weather changed overnight, the temperatures rising sharply, the sky a clear pale blue day after day. And each day the sun's warmth seemed a little more convincing.

In the fields that surrounded the house the snow melted with dramatic speed, although deep pockets still remained in the woods, and would until June. Even the snowman was only an untidy white heap. By the side of the house tiny spears of green appeared through last year's dead grass and the buds on the willows began to thicken. The fox sparrows arrived, resting for a few days on their long migratory flight; they shuffled through the seeds that had fallen to the ground from Vicki's bird feeder, their feathers mottled rust and grey in the sun. At dawn and dusk the white-tailed deer emerged from the forest to feed, their dull flanks thin from the winter's scant foraging.

As though nature's stirring to life had infected her, Vicki found herself recalling every detail of the time Stephen and Garth had spent with her. She had meant to forget them, to push the brief visit out of her mind as though it had never existed, but she soon discovered this was impossible. Each time she went to the shed Stephen's vivid little face accompanied her, his shrill, piping voice carrying through the trees. When she sat down to eat, Garth was across from her, quizzical grey eyes fastened on her face, deep voice challenging her, warm hands resting on her wrists.

For the first time since she had moved to the shore, she began seriously to question the future. She had enough money saved up for a year here, if she lived fairly frugally. She had started a children's book, an adventure story set on the sea coast, illustrated with her own line drawings; she alternated between being sure it showed both talent and promise, to being equally sure it was no good at all and would never be published. What she did know was that she loved doing it, and it was this that made her persevere. A career as a writer—was that what she wanted? If her books *were* published, would that be enough? She saw herself ten years in the future, living alone, with no man to care for her, no child to brighten her days . . . and then she would remember the unhappy months with Barry. She had fallen in love with him and married him, only to find out that he had deceived her and used her. Her disillusion had been so total, her misery so all-pervading, that she had vowed never to trust anyone again or to let anyone close to her. Because of this vow, she had sent Garth and Stephen away.

She had half expected to hear from them, but the slow days passed without any sign of them and she began to realise that she had succeeded in her aim. She should have been pleased. But she was not.

Because of a restlessness and a loneliness that were too deep to ignore, she spent more time with Nils, and if he wondered about the frequency of her visits, he forbore to say anything, accepting her presence with an outward lack of surprise that she appreciated. She helped him mend his nets, her fingers nimble with the pointed bone needle. She painted the styrofoam buoys in broad stripes of orange and black, the colours that would distinguish his lobster traps from those of the other fishermen. She painted the underside of the dory. The day after he set his traps, she went out to help him haul them. As trap after trap was brought up from the ocean bottom by the winch, emptied of its precious cargo of lobster and baited again with herring, Nils grew steadily more and more exultant. Finally the last trap splashed back into the sea, its bright buoy bobbing on the waves. 'Close on five hundred pounds,' he said, stretching his back and arms. 'That's a darn good haul. Let's hope it keeps up now for the rest of the season.'

Vicki knew what a chancy business lobster fishing could be and she was pleased for him. 'Is that all of them now?'

'Yeah. I'll go out later and check the herring nets. Lordy, it's cold, isn't it?' He accelerated the boat and in a swirl of wake headed for the shore, with its line of surf rolling up the beach, and its craggy grey cliffs, topped with thick, dark evergreens. 'Been meaning to ask you,' he yelled above the engine's roar and the slap of water on the prow, 'did you hear anything more from Garth and Stephen?'

The question took her off balance. 'No—nothing,' she shouted back.

She missed the flicker of relief in his blue eyes.

'Strange—I'd have thought he'd have been in touch. You know, I'm sure I've seen him somewhere before, but I'm darned if I know where. I've been trying to remember all week. Here, you steer, and I'll clean out the bait bucket.' Vicki took the wheel, peering through the salt-spattered glass at the shoreline, her mind intent on the task.

In a few minutes Nils came and stood beside her. 'Hold her steady—that's good. I haven't figured out why you didn't want him to know the truth about Barry.'

Vicki shifted uncomfortably. 'It was more or less instinctive, I think, Nils. I found him—dangerous. Overbearing, maybe—certainly used to getting his own way. At any rate, a very strong personality.'

'Still running, eh, Vicki?'

She had told Nils something of her background, although by no means all. 'It's not running at all,' she retorted. 'It's just being reasonable and looking after my own interests.'

'Huh,' he grunted disbelievingly, but being Nils did not pursue it any farther. 'Better let me take over now.' With a skill acquired over the years he brought *Seafoam* into her mooring at the wharf. Clumsy with the cold, Vicky scrambled up the ladder, caught the hawser and looped it around the iron ring which was sunk in one of the creosoted beams. She straightened, wincing a little from a crick in her back.

A man had been watching their arrival from the shelter of the fish shed. Now he stepped out into the open, his eyes fastened on the girl. The wind caught her hair, whipping it around her head, and tugged at her yellow oilskin jacket; her cheeks were red with cold.

From the corner of her eye she sensed his approach. She turned. Walking towards her was a tall, dark-haired man, with eyes as grey as the ocean. Garth. . . .

CHAPTER FOUR

Her mind blank, Vicki waited for Garth to say something, but as he came level with her he only halted for a moment, his expression inscrutable, his features set. Then he walked past her and called down to Nils, 'Need a hand?'

Nils straightened slowly, his eyes narrow slits. 'Sure,' he said expressionlessly. 'I've got close on five hundred pounds of lobster to load in the truck and take to the pound. Here, grab this.'

Her cheeks flushed with more than the cold, for Garth's detached scrutiny had angered her, Vicki watched the two men bring the wooden crates ashore and load them on Nils's half-ton truck. As Nils got behind the wheel, he called out, 'Thanks, Vicki. See you later,' before driving the truck up the dirt track, the wheels shooting rocks out behind.

A dark green Rover was parked near the fish shed. 'Get in,' Garth ordered.

Vicki did not move, her lips set stubbornly. 'Where are we going?'

'To your place.'

She did not seem to have any choice. 'I smell of fish,' she said defiantly.

'Get in, Vicki.'

There was no arguing with that tone of voice. She did as she was told, rubbing her cold hands together in her lap as in silence they drove the short distance to the farmhouse. At the back door she hung up her jacket and pulled off her boots; underneath she was wearing jeans and a thick gold sweater that lightened her eyes to amber.

'I'll look after the furnace if you want to start the kitchen stove,' Garth said levelly.

In frustrated silence Vicki shoved paper and kindling into the stove and held a match to them. But then her

46

anger vanished, swallowed up in a gathering anxiety. Why had he come back? What did he want of her? Nothing pleasant, judging by his manner. She added some split birch logs to the leaping flames, closed the stove door and went to wash her hands. They were red and chafed, and she was smoothing some hand-cream on them when Garth came upstairs.

'Weren't you wearing gloves?' he asked.

'Yes, I was. But they got soaked through while we were hauling the traps.' Even as she spoke, she was conscious of a sense of total unreality—he had not come a hundred miles for this kind of small talk.

He took her hands between his and rubbed them briskly until the warmth from his fingers spread to hers and the redness was gone. It seemed to take a long time, the girl thought, her eyes fastened on the intricate pattern of his Aran sweater; she found she could not meet his eyes. Finally he said, 'There, that's better.' But instead of releasing her, he brought one of her hands up to his cheek and held it there.

She saw the pink ovals of her nails against the tanned skin; she could feel the hard bone, the silkiness of his dark hair. For a crazy moment she wanted to run her fingers through his hair and pull his head down ... aghast, she snatched her hand away.

'What's wrong?' he asked.

'I've told you before, I don't like to be touched.'

His eyes narrowed. 'Do you say that to your husband?'

'No!' she retorted. 'Why should I?'

'Why should you indeed?' he repeated smoothly. 'I never did credit you with the ability to communicate beyond the grave.'

Her mouth went dry. 'What are you talking about?'

'I'm talking about your husband. Who's been dead and buried for over a year.'

Like those of a trapped animal, her eyes flew to the door. 'No, Vicki,' said Garth, guessing her intentions immediately. 'You're through with running away. We're going to have this out.'

The second person today to accuse her of running away. 'How did you find out about Barry?' Vicki asked.

'A friend of mine's a lawyer—he got me the information I needed.' He added grimly, 'I'm glad you're not wasting time trying to deny it. It was all lies, wasn't it, Vicki? The devoted husband, who was away. The faithful wife waiting at home for him. Just a pack of lies!'

His voice had risen and only by considerable effort did she keep herself from shrinking away from him. 'Not all of it,' she said quietly.

'And just how is one supposed to separate the wheat from the chaff?' he said sarcastically.

'Barry *is* dead,' she said with as much dignity as she could muster. 'I lied to you about that. But it doesn't really make much difference, you know——'

'It makes all the difference in the world!' he interrupted furiously. 'Don't you understand? I thought you were married—how the hell could I have any kind of relationship with you under those circumstances? And now I've found out you're not. It makes all the difference in the world,' he repeated, his grey eyes blazing.

'To you maybe—but not to me!' Her voice was cutting.

He grew very still. 'Just what do you mean by that?'

'I don't know what you have in mind when you talk about relationships, but whatever it is, I'm not interested.'

'Are you thinking I just want to have an affair with you, is that it?'

He looked angry enough to pick her up and shake her. 'How am I supposed to know what you want?' she snapped.

Garth fought for control, taking two or three deep steadying breaths. 'Look,' he said, 'let's sit down and discuss this reasonably. Why don't you put the kettle on and make a cup of tea?'

Stubbornly Vicki stood her ground. 'I don't think we have anything to discuss.'

Abruptly he was on his feet again, towering over her. 'That's where you're wrong, Vicki. First of all there's the fact that you deliberately lied to me about your marriage and I want to know why. Secondly, there's the fact that I want to marry you. I think we've plenty to discuss.'

This time it was she who sat down, for her legs would no longer hold her up. 'Marry me?' she repeated faintly.

'That's what I said.'

'You don't even know me!'

'I know everything that matters.'

'You can't possibly. . . .'

'Didn't you hear a word I said to you last week?' he asked, his voice suddenly gentle. 'To start with, there's your beauty—well, that's obvious.' He saw her instinctive move of denial and said softly, 'You should see yourself now—your hair a tangle of silk, your cheeks flushed from the sea wind to the colour of a wild rose, your eyes like dark woodland pools, full of mystery. . . .'

His words hypnotised her, banishing the conflict between them, and suddenly there was a new confidence in the tilt of her chin and a glow of pride in those dark eyes.

'You're beginning to believe me, aren't you?'

She smiled shyly. 'Yes, I think I am.'

'I don't understand how you could have looked in a mirror all these years and not have seen what I see. And it's a beauty that will be with you until the day you die—your bone structure is exquisite. . . .'

Unaccustomed warmth curled around her heart, as deep within her a hurt that went back as far as she could remember began to loosen its hold.

'Tell me what you're thinking,' he said softly.

She owed him at least that much. Looking back over the years, her eyes lost in memory, she said, 'It's a commonplace enough story. My parents died when I was very young and I went to live with my aunt and uncle on their farm in New Brunswick. They had no children of their own. But I wasn't a very good substitute. To start with, I wasn't a boy. Just a girl—not completely useless but not really much good. I worked my heart out for them, trying to get their approval—just for once. Of course I never did.' She gazed down at her hands loosely clasped on the tablecloth. 'Now that I'm older, I can recognise that they were mean-spirited people—no love in them, no laughter or joy. They always expected the worst to happen, and so of course often it did. But at the time I was too involved and I didn't understand at all. I only knew I was miserable and that no matter what I did, it was never enough. They always referred to me as a skinny little thing . . . a pity she's so ugly, they'd say to visitors. So perhaps, with them, I was ugly. . . .'

'What happened to them?'

'They both died in a 'flu epidemic when I was sixteen. I got out of there as fast as I could and moved to Montreal.'

'And you've been carrying the scars around ever since.'

She smiled wryly. 'I guess you're right.'

'But not any more.' There was a question in his look.

Seriously she said, 'I'll try not to.'

'Good girl!' he grinned. 'Now where was I? Oh yes, the reasons why I want to marry you——'

Her breath caught in her throat. 'Please, Garth——'

'Vicki, you're a widow. You're free to marry me.'

She gave an angry laugh. 'Legally, I suppose you're right. But that doesn't make much difference, because I shall never marry again, Garth.'

'Why not?' His eyes were like two stones.

'My marriage with Barry didn't work out. I won't risk that happening again.'

'Come on, Vicki, you've got to do better than that. Of all people, I should know you're not a coward.'

The lamplight fell over his face, and she missed none of the ruthlessness in the hard grey eyes and the straight gash of a mouth. 'You can call it cowardice if you like— I'd rather call it ordinary common sense. Once bitten, twice shy—haven't you ever heard that? In my case it happens to be true.'

He directed at her all the force of his personality. 'With me it would be different,' he said.

'I have no way of knowing that, do I? Except to marry you, of course—and that I will not do.' The air between them was vibrating with tension and she made an effort to bring things back to some kind of normality. 'This whole conversation is crazy, Garth. You spent twenty-four hours in my house two weeks ago and now you walk in and say you want to marry me. You can't expect me to take that seriously.'

'Time is a relative thing—I knew as soon as I saw you that I wanted you.' As she made a move to speak, he added, 'Be quiet a minute and listen. I know you're not indifferent to me——'

She could not stop herself interrupting. 'How?'

'Because you lied to me—why should you bother unless I represented some kind of a threat to you? You never lied to Nils, did you?'

Vicki glared at him in frustration. Once again he was right. 'This isn't getting us anywhere,' she said coldly. 'Apart from anything else, do you realise I know scarcely anything about you? I don't even know what you do for a living or where you live.'

'Those are minor details,' he said impatiently. 'I'm well able to support you, if that's what you're worrying about.'

'Of course it's not,' she retorted. 'Look, I've had enough. You've asked me to marry you—at least I think you have—and I've said no. So that's that.'

'Not quite, no.' Not until he spoke did she realise just how hard he was fighting back anger. 'Let me tell you something else. Stephen misses you—I've never known him to take to anyone the way he did to you. He needs a mother, Vicki. A woman to love him and to look after him.'

'That's blackmail!' she gasped.

'No, it's not—it's the simple truth.'

'I can't help you, Garth. Not you, or your son. I won't make that kind of commitment again.'

'What in God's name did Barry do to you?'

Her face closed. 'That's my business.'

She watched his fists clench on the tablecloth, knowing that his level voice when he spoke was the result of a supreme effort of will. 'Do at least this much for us, Vicki. Come and stay with us for a few days. Call it a holiday if you like. I promise not to pressure you while you're there, not to try and make you talk about Barry if you don't want to.'

'No!' she spat, knowing even as she spoke that she was tempted . . . to see Stephen again and have time to play with him, to bring that vivid smile to his face and feel his thin little body hurtling against hers . . . yes, she wanted that. But what of this man, Stephen's father? It was playing with fire to even contemplate spending more time with him. . . . 'No,' she repeated more quietly. 'It's useless, Garth.'

'So you won't even do it for Stephen's sake?'

She bit her lip. 'No,' she said, so faintly that the word was hardly audible.

'You really are a selfish little bitch, aren't you?' he said conversationally.

'I'm not!'

'Yes, you are. You're so damned wrapped up in your own troubles that you just can't see that anyone else has needs at all. You know,' he went on in just the same tone of voice, 'all I'd have to do is pick you up and put you in the car and then you wouldn't have any choice, would you?'

He was quite capable of carrying out his threat, she knew. 'When Harold did that, you called it kidnapping.'

'Don't push me, Vicki, or I might just do it.'

She was beginning to feel very tired. 'I think you'd better go now,' she said evenly. 'This isn't serving much purpose, is it?'

He got up slowly, stretching to his full height. 'Before I go, I think I should kiss you goodbye, don't you?' he said, grinning wolfishly. 'After all, it may be my only chance.'

She was suddenly conscious of their isolation, of the silence of the house and of the larger silence of the woods and fields around them. 'I don't think that's necessary,' she said, also getting up and holding on to the back of her chair. 'Goodbye, Garth.'

He came round the table so that he was between her and the door, and like some petrified wild creature, she was rooted to the spot. Deliberately he rested his hands on her shoulders, curving his fingers around her fragile bones, holding her imprisoned with ridiculous ease. 'Please let go,' she whispered.

'It's my turn to say no—this time you're not getting your own way.' By increasing the pressure of his hands he drew her closer to him. She could see the rise and fall of his chest, the corded muscles of his neck and the taut, unforgiving line of his jaw. He was paralysingly close and her heart was beating so fast she thought she would suffocate. If it had been possible to will herself to faint, she would have done so, but instead everything seemed bathed in a peculiar clarity: the intricate cable stitching on his sweater; the clean soap-and-water smell of his skin, undeniably masculine; the bite of his fingernails in her shoulders. Helplessly she raised her head.

With the steel strength of a trap, his arms went around her, pulling her to him so that they stood body to body. She had managed to slide her palms against his chest, but although she pushed away from him with all her strength, she might as well have saved herself the trouble; he held her immobile. 'Let me go!'

'When I'm ready. . . .' He lowered his head and his mouth closed on hers.

For a brief instant she was still in his arms. Then her mind convulsed with panic and her whole body recoiled. Wriggling, kicking, striking his chest with her fists, she fought to be free. But his arms only tightened their hold, one hand at her waist, the other against her shoulderblades, and inexorably his mouth moved against hers, smothering any outcry she might have made.

She worked her hands free—she'd scratch his face or pull his hair, she thought fiercely, in that moment as different from the normally cool, controlled Vicki as day from night. One hand slid up his neck and her fingers found the soft curls at his nape, the other reached up to his cheek.

Under her palms his skin was smooth and warm. The shock of pleasure that raced through her body was like a jolt of electricity; suddenly she went limp in his arms. Her fingers moved in his hair, burying themselves in it, probing his scalp, as guided by instinct rather than experience, her lips parted under his and sweetness flooded her body. Her body grew pliant against his lean hips and the hard breadth of his chest. Never in her life had she felt this ache of longing, this languorous, pulsing desire, and as fiercely as she had fought Garth a few moments ago, she now surrendered to him.

When he roughly thrust her away, her eyes flew open—tawny eyes, gold with the awakening of passion. Her cheeks were flushed, her lips warm and soft from his kisses, and from her face the wonderment had not yet faded.

His grey eyes were alight with such a blaze of emotion that she felt the first return of panic. She swallowed, trying desperately to get hold of herself. When he had pushed her away, she had landed up against the table, and now she gripped its edges, holding tight on to something solid and real, for in a few brief moments this man had turned her safe little world upside down. 'Garth . . .?' she said tentatively.

'Don't worry, I won't do it again,' he snarled. As he picked up the car keys from the table, she saw with secret amazement that his fingers were unsteady. So not only she had been affected by that kiss. . . . She opened her mouth to tell him she had changed her mind, that she would go with him to Seal Cove, but before she could speak, he said violently, 'Maybe that will give you something to think about when you lie alone here, night after night. And let me give you something else to think about—it was Stephen's idea that you come for a visit. I'm going to have to go home now and tell him you won't come. I hope you're proud of yourself, Vicki.'

She paled, the golden radiance vanishing from her eyes. 'Garth, I——'

'Goodbye, Vicki. And this *is* goodbye.'

The door slammed behind him and seconds later she

heard the roar of his car engine. Galvanised into life, she stumbled to the front door, but she was too late—the car was already turning on to the highway and with a mocking squeal of tires was out of sight behind the trees.

She leaned her forehead against the windowpane, not even noticing the coldness of the glass, wondering with a strange sense of detachment if she was going to faint now—now that he was gone. However, the dizziness passed, although she felt ice-cold and her knees were trembling uncontrollably. Feeling her way like a blind person, she sank down on the chesterfield, and for a long time stared sightlessly at the opposite wall. With painful honesty she relived every moment of that devastating kiss, during which her emotions had run the gamut from terror to anger to what she now knew was desire. She had wanted the kiss to continue; it had been like an amputation when Garth had pushed her away. She closed her eyes, remembering the pressure of his hands on her hips, the hardness of his chest, the fierce demand of his mouth, and her body leaped into life and her blood throbbed with primitive needs she had never known existed.

Slowly she got up and walked over to the window, looking out over the bare fields. There was a dusting of green in the hollows and over by the brook the silver blur of pussy willows. Birds carolled in the trees. The earth, after its long winter, was awakening to the sun, stirring to life. Garth had said there would be no spring for her— but he had been wrong. One kiss from him and the ice had started to melt from her frozen heart, and her body, like the earth, was stirring from its long slumber. She remembered the line of poetry that had claimed April as the cruellest month and for the first time she began to understand what that meant: a vulnerability to desires beyond her control, a hope that somehow love would catch her up and carry her beyond herself into a summer of warmth of fruition . . . but she had sent Garth away. And Garth was a proud man, she knew—he would not come begging again. She had sent him away, and now she must live with the consequences. Loneliness, and the

haunting, bittersweet knowledge of something that might
have been. . . .

One kiss from Garth was all it had taken. Yet she had
lived with Barry for months and she had felt nothing like
that flooding of emotion she had just experienced. She
had loved Barry—hadn't she? She had been in love with
him when she married him, or so she had thought at the
time. Perhaps it was nothing to do with love, she decided
confusedly. For she certainly did not love Garth Travis.
She would be better off if she never saw him again—
which, of course, was a very likely prospect. That she
should feel depression settle on her, just as mist would
settle on the hills, was beyond her understanding.

Three days later she awoke to fog as a reality: a thick
white mist pushing at the windows and shrouding the
house in silence. Knowing Nils would not be able to go
out to his traps until it cleared, she busied herself around
the house. Just before lunch she went outdoors to put
more seed in the bird feeder; all winter she had kept it
stocked with seed, enjoying the sight of so many different
woodland birds: greedy blue jays, colourful finches and
grosbeaks, shy pine siskins. The little black-capped chick-
adees were used to her now, and as she stood by the feeder
two of them hopped on the tray and began pecking at the
seeds. Amused by their air of cheery unconcern, she
watched them for several minutes until suddenly they both
flew away in a whirr of wings. Something must have
startled them. She turned to go back to the house and
through the fog she heard the muffled sound of footsteps on
the gravel driveway. It was an eerie sensation, hearing but
not seeing, and she called out uncertainly, 'Who's there?'

A small figure materialised from the mist. 'Stephen!'
she exclaimed. 'What on earth are you doing here?'

He halted a few feet away from her. His schoolbag was
looped over the shoulders of his yellow rain-slicker and
his hair curled damply. He was obviously not sure of his
welcome. 'Hi, Vicki.'

Vicki said the first thing that came into her head. 'Why

aren't you in school?'

'I came to see you instead.'

'Does your father know you're here?'

'No.'

'Stephen, I don't understand—how did you get here?'

'I caught the bus.'

'But why?'

Her volley of questions made him step back a pace. 'I wanted to see you,' he said, his voice not quite steady.

In swift compunction Vicki replied, 'You look cold and wet, dear. Come inside and you can explain what's up.'

In the porch she hung up his schoolbag and took off his coat, then led him into the kitchen. 'How about a bowl of soup and a sandwich?' she said matter-of-factly. 'I made some cookies this morning, too.'

Not until they were seated at the table and Stephen was tucking into his lunch with all the appetite of a normal small boy did she say, 'Won't your father be wondering where you are?'

'No—he thinks I'm at school. But instead of getting on the school bus, I got on the bus to Sydney.' He added reassuringly, 'I used my own money. I had some saved up.'

Trying to understand, she asked, 'You wanted to see me that much? Or did you just want a day off school?'

'No—I wanted to see you. Dad said you wouldn't come for a visit, but I thought he couldn't have tried very hard to make you come.'

Unaccountably Vicki blushed under his clear-eyed scrutiny. 'Oh,' she said weakly.

'You *will* come, won't you?' This in between large bites of home-made bread, and uttered with complete confidence.

'Your father may not want me now,' she murmured.

'Sure he will.'

She couldn't help laughing at his convincing air of wisdom. 'Be that as it may,' she said warmly, 'you really shouldn't have come, Stephen. Not without your father knowing.'

'If I'd told him, he wouldn't have let me come.'

This was irrefutable logic. 'I suppose not,' she said, trying not very successfully to look stern. 'What time are you supposed to get home from school?'

'Ten past three.'

'Two hours from now—we'll have to phone him, Stephen, and let him know you're here. He'll be angry, won't he?'

'Prob'ly.'

She wished she could be as philosophical as he about it. 'When you've finished eating, we'll go to Nils's and borrow his truck. I don't feel like walking four miles to the phone.' She hesitated, then decided to take the plunge. 'Stephen, I'm still not quite sure I understand why you're here. It's sweet of you to want me to visit you, but to come so far just for that. Especially when you know you're going to get in trouble for doing it.'

He finished chewing a mouthful of sandwich. He was wearing a dark grey sweater over his jeans; the sweater, she noticed, needed darning. As he fiddled with the handle of his knife, avoiding her eyes, she also thought he looked overly pale for a boy who spent a lot of time outdoors. Finally he burst out, 'All the other boys have mothers and I don't. I thought if you came and stayed for a while, I could pretend you were my mother.'

She was aghast. This went deeper than she had thought. 'I don't think you can pretend something like that, Stephen,' she said gently. 'You had a real mother—I can never take her place.'

'I guess not,' he said slowly, and it was almost as though she could sense his conflicting loyalties. 'But I wouldn't miss her as much if you were there.' He glanced at Vicki shyly through thick dark lashes that were very like his father's. ' 'Cause I like you. You're sensible—you know about stuff like cutting up wood and making fires. And you're not always telling me I mustn't get dirty.'

Although she was both touched and amused, she persisted, 'But if I came for a visit, Stephen, it would be just that—sooner or later I'd have to come home.'

'Maybe you'd like it so much you'd stay.'

'Oh, Stephen. . . .' He had it all worked out. Not knowing what to say, she got up to fetch him some cookies and milk. He carried his plate over to the sink and on impulse she suddenly dropped to her knees and hugged him. He flung his arms around her, burying his face in her sweater. 'No matter what happens,' she said unsteadily, 'I'm really pleased that you thought enough of me to come here. Okay?'

'Okay. And if it's all right with Dad, you'll come and stay with us?'

'Yes.' The word came out on its own volition. She was committed now, she thought dazedly. Somehow this small boy with his clear eyes and sooty lashes had found his way through all her defences. He needed her to give him something he was lacking, something every boy should have—a woman's care.

Her heart gave a sudden jolt of dismay. But what of his father? She was forgetting Garth's reaction to all this. After their last meeting, she was probably the last person he wanted to see again—let alone have as a guest in his house. She remembered the uncompromising chin and hard grey eyes and momentarily gave way to despair. 'You must try not to be disappointed if your father decides against this visit, Stephen.'

The small chin was thrust out. 'He'd better not.'

She said diplomatically, 'Come and dry the dishes and then we'll walk to the cabin.'

Obediently he picked up the towel. 'We have a dishwasher at home,' he remarked.

'I see.' She added curiously, 'What does your father do, Stephen? For a living, I mean.'

'He writes books.'

'Oh? What kind of books?'

'Novels. He calls himself Paul Tarrant when he writes.'

Her voice rose incredulously. 'Paul Tarrant is your father?'

'Mmm—you know about him?'

'Of course I do! Who doesn't? He's one of Canada's

best known writers.' She tried to digest the astonishing fact that the famous Paul Tarrant had stayed in her house, eaten at her table—kissed her. Her mind boggled. 'What on earth is he doing living here? I'd have thought Toronto or Vancouver would have been more his style.'

'We lived in Toronto for a long time. But we moved here last year. Dad said he'd had enough of the city. He wanted to be able to go out on his front steps in the morning and take a deep breath without being—sphixated, or something.'

'Asphixiated, I think you mean,' she said, amusement conquering her amazement. 'Well, I'm sure you can do that at Seal Cove. There, we're finished. Let's go to Nils's.' Together they left the house and began to walk down the driveway towards the road.

CHAPTER FIVE

A COUPLE of hours later Vicki and Stephen arrived back at the house, the arrangement having been made by telephone that Garth would come and get Stephen. Stephen certainly didn't seem to be worrying about Garth's reaction to his escapade, Vicki noticed; she herself was aware of a tightening of her nerves as the time came nearer for Garth's arrival.

In an effort to distract herself, she left Stephen outdoors playing and went into her bedroom, thoughtfully considering the contents of her wardrobe; perhaps it would help if she changed into something other than jeans. She had got rid of everything Barry had bought her—a lot of it with her own money, of course—but she still had several outfits from the days before his whirlwind courtship. She finally settled on a flared plaid skirt in shades of green and beige and an off-white turtleneck pullover made of soft, fluffy angora. She gathered her hair into a loose knot on the top of her head, then applied a touch of green eyeshadow and mascara to her eyes, and a soft apricot lipstick to her lips. Gravely she looked at herself in the mirror, her eyes full of uncertainty. Would Garth think she looked beautiful today? And why should it matter to her whether he did or not?

In the kitchen she quickly put the fish chowder on to heat and set the table, putting out a basket of fresh rolls and some of Nils's homemade butter. She was just completing her preparations when she heard a car approaching the house, and from outside Stephen's, 'Hi, Dad.' Then there was the slam of a car door and the low murmur of Garth's voice, interspersed with occasional high-pitched interruptions from Stephen. Finally she heard the back door open and the clump of boots being removed, and then a rather chastened-looking Stephen came into the kitchen, Garth on his heels. Before Vicki could say anything, Stephen stopped in his tracks and said, 'Wow! You look pretty, Vicki. Eh, Dad?'

Garth's eyes were trained on the slim figure standing by the table, with her high crown of dark silky hair that looked almost too heavy for the slender neck. 'She does indeed,' he said, and Vicki was quite unable to deduce what emotion, if any, lay behind the quietly spoken words.

She felt overcome by a paralysing shyness. The dark-haired man who filled her doorway was none other than Paul Tarrant, an acclaimed writer, a man who characteristically moved in circles far removed from hers. A sophisticated, knowledgeable man, whose books about contemporary life showed discernment, a piercing intelligence, and a sense of compassion she had always admired. What on earth could she find to say to him?

'What are you staring at me like that for?' he demanded, an edge to his voice.

She flushed and blurted, 'I'm sorry. You see, I only found out today that you're Paul Tarrant—I didn't know.'

'What difference does it make?' he said irritably. 'I'm still Garth Travis, aren't I? I might as well tell you that I loathe being lionised.'

Her eyes widened. In a quick flash of insight she saw exactly what he meant: as Paul Tarrant, a famous man of letters, he must be treated anything but naturally. Her shyness vanished. Her smile broke through and she said quickly, 'I won't do that, I promise! But I would like you to know that your books have given me a great deal of pleasure.'

He inclined his head and she sensed he was pleased with her reply. 'Thank you, Vicki.'

'Now,' she said briskly, 'how about something to eat? Stephen, wash your hands, dear. How was the driving, Garth—bad, because of the fog?'

The conversation remained on neutral ground throughout the meal. Once the dishes were cleared away,

Garth said abruptly, 'Stephen, I need to talk privately with Vicki. We'll go for a walk around the field—you'll be all right here for a few minutes, won't you?'

The little boy nodded, flashing a pleading look in Vicki's direction. She smiled at him with all the reassurance at her command, before slipping a slicker over her jacket and changing her shoes for boots.

In the dusk the mist curled wraith-like over the wet grass. They tramped across the field until they came to the gnarled old apple tree that many years ago must have been part of a flourishing orchard. Needing support, Vicki leaned against the trunk and a shower of droplets fell on her hair, caught there like tiny diamonds. The house had disappeared in the fog; she and Garth could have been alone in the world. As she waited for him to speak, she studied him covertly. His beige cavalry trousers emphasised his long legs and lean hips; a heavy lumberman's jacket over an open-necked shirt, and high laced leather boots completed his outfit. He looked at the same time capable, rakish, and tough. Behind them from the spruce trees the silence was broken by a harsh outcry of crows and overhead there came a disembodied beat of heavy wings. Vicki shivered, for it seemed a bad omen.

'Cold?'

'No, it's all right,' she said. 'Someone walking over my grave.'

'Just what has Stephen been saying to you?'

She pulled a piece of bark from one of the branches and began systematically tearing it to shreds. Sparing Garth nothing, she said evenly, 'He told me he was different from all the other boys because he didn't have a mother.'

She heard him catch his breath sharply. 'And I suppose he sees you as a likely candidate?'

She shrank from the brutality of his tone, but bravely raising her eyes to his. 'Yes. At the risk of sounding conceited, he says he really likes me.' Unconsciously her mouth softened as she remembered Stephen's somewhat unconventional list of her virtues.

'And you like him?'

'I like him very much,' she said with complete honesty.

Garth scuffed the rocky ground with his steel-toed boot. 'I didn't know he minded that there were just the two of us—he's never said anything about it before.' There did not seem to be anything she could say to this, so she remained silent. 'Did he tell you anything about Corinne—his mother?'

There was something in his voice she had never heard before—a strain, a long-held unhappiness; and tragedy brushed her like the black wings of a crow. He still loved her, Vicki thought numbly. Corinne, who had been the mother of his son, whose death Harold had set out to avenge. . . . She fought for control, her nails digging into the tree trunk. 'All he said was that he still missed her.'

'I see.' A wealth of bitterness in the two short words.

She felt a wave of compassion and impulsively put her hand on his sleeve. 'Garth, in a sense that doesn't matter at all, because I made it quite clear to Stephen that there was no way I could replace his real mother. But I do have a suggestion of a way we might work it out—that is, if you're interested?'

He looked down at the slim, competent fingers resting on his sleeve and said with startling irrelevance, 'What did you do with your wedding ring?'

She snatched her hand away. 'I sold it.'

'*Sold* it?' She nodded, hot colour staining her cheeks. 'Why?'

'I needed the money,' she said tersely. 'Besides, I had no desire to keep it.'

'Your marriage was that bad?'

'Garth, this has nothing to do with Stephen!'

'It might have everything to do with it.' His eyes narrowed and he took a step towards her, crowding her against the trunk. 'I understand from Stephen you might be willing to come to Seal Cove—why the change of heart, Vicki? A couple of days ago there was nothing I could do or say to persuade you to come.'

She swallowed. 'I guess I realised today after talking to

Stephen how much he does need a woman around.'

'So you'll come for his sake—but not for mine.'

Danger ... her nerves quivered with a warning that could only be instinctive. 'That's right. If I come, Garth, it would have to be clearly understood that it's strictly as a companion for Stephen. Nothing else.'

'So what are you going to do—pretend that I don't exist?'

'You haven't heard my suggestion yet,' she said, her mouth dry.

'Very well.' He moved back a step and for the first time it occurred to her that this interview was being as great a strain on him as on her—but why?

'Why don't I come as your housekeeper rather than as your guest——' She checked his move to interrupt. 'Hear me out. We'll make it a business arrangement. A two-week trial period, or something like that. And then if it's not satisfactory to all three of us, I can come back home. It would be easier to deal with on that basis, don't you agree?'

'And what salary were you thinking of?'

She gasped audibly. 'I don't want a salary at all! You can keep your money. I'm doing this as a favour for Stephen. I just thought it would be better to put it on a more businesslike footing, that's all.'

'I see. So the fact that you've found out I'm the famous—and rich—Paul Tarrant has nothing to do with your change of heart?'

She was suddenly no longer afraid of him, and as her temper flared she made no effort to control it. 'Damn you, Garth Travis! You do persist in putting the worst interpretation on everything I say and do, don't you? If you think I'm that kind of a snob, you can hardly consider me a fit companion for your son. In which case the deal's off, anyway.'

It was ironic that he should have so misconstrued her motives. His double identity as Paul Tarrant was a hindrance rather than an attraction, for now she felt she would have to keep hidden from him her aspirations as a writer.

'When you lose your temper, your eyes are almost gold—do you know that? They looked that way after I kissed you, too.' He leaned forward, his palms against the trunk over her head. As she stayed frozen to the spot, with deliberate sensuality he brushed his lips across her forehead and down her cheek until he found her mouth. His kiss was deep, demanding a response from her. Vicki held herself rigid, her mouth unmoving and unresponsive, and it took every ounce of her will power and all of her strength. His lips probed, quested, sought . . . deep within her a flame burst to life and desperately she tamped it down; she could not have said whether she was fighting him or herself.

It was the harsh cry of the crows that brought her back to her senses. Earlier they had warned her of danger . . . violently she twisted her head free, her breath sobbing in her throat. 'Don't, Garth!'

His eyes burned like coals. 'You're coming to Seal Cove for Stephen. But you're coming for me as well——'

'No!'

'Vicki, you're as attracted to me as I am to you—you just won't be honest about it.'

'I'm not! I swear I'm not——'

'Don't try and tell me you don't want me to kiss you, because I won't believe you.'

'I don't give a damn whether you believe me or not!' she cried. 'Just leave me alone.'

'So you can sleep away the rest of your life?'

'That's my decision, isn't it? If I'm going to look after Stephen, you must promise to keep your hands off me.'

'I'll make no promises of any kind, Vicki Peters. I won't have conditions put on my behaviour in my own house.'

The chill, damp air seemed to have penetrated to her bones. Nothing would make him back down, she knew. So the choice was hers—to go to Seal Cove or to stay here. If she stayed, she was the one who would have to try and explain her change of heart to Stephen and face his inevitable disillusionment. If she went, there would be conflict and risk and storms ahead. Even now, and in

spite of her inner battle, her body tingled with an awareness of his nearness; equally she longed for and feared his
kisses. But after all, she argued inwardly, there could be
no parallel to the relationship with Barry, for she had
been in love with Barry and it was love that had betrayed
her. She would never love this harsh-faced, arrogant
stranger.

'I shall come to Seal Cove,' she said clearly.

If she had been expecting effusive thanks, she was to be
disappointed. All he did was to nod slowly, as though she
had confirmed something to him. 'Good. Let's go and tell
Stephen.'

Stephen's reaction, at least, was all Vicki could have
wanted. He threw his arms around her so hard that she
staggered. 'Will you make chocolate cake?' he demanded.
'And can I have my friends in after school to have some?'

'Yes, I will, and yes, you can,' she laughed.

'How long will it take you to pack?' Garth asked. 'We
should get going very soon—Stephen has school tomorrow.'

'Oh, I can't go tonight,' she said in faint dismay.

'Why not?' he snapped. 'Not changing your mind
already, are you?'

She shot him a look that spoke volumes, but for
Stephen's benefit said dulcetly, 'Of course not. But it will
take a few hours to get myself organised—I'll have to
drain the water pipes, and ask Nils to keep the chickens
and a few things like that. I could catch the bus tomorrow
afternoon.'

'No, I'll come for you,' said Garth decisively. 'What
time—one o'clock?'

Feeling as though she was being swept along by an
irresistible current, Vicki said, 'All right—if I'm not here,
I'll be at Nils's delivering the chickens.'

'Fine.' He glanced down at Stephen. 'So we'll both be
home tomorrow when you get back from school.'

'We'll both be home. . . .' This phrase brought a little
stab of pleasure to Vicki's heart. To share a home, a real
home . . . how lovely that would be. She never really had

had that opportunity before. Certainly the luxurious, ultra-modern apartment she and Barry had rented in Montreal had not been a home. A place where they occasionally met. A place to impress his friends. A place to give parties which she gradually came to dread. But never a home.

'Come back to earth, Vicki.'

She blinked and the shadows lifted from her eyes. 'Sorry,' she muttered. Patting Stephen on the shoulder, she said, 'I'll see you after school, then. I may not get the chocolate cake made tomorrow, but I promise I will the next day.'

'Cross your heart and hope to die.'

Solemnly she went through the ritual, crossing both hands on her breast and only then realising how closely Garth was watching her. She snatched her fingers away, her cheeks pink, and heard him say, 'Goodnight, Vicki. One o'clock tomorrow.' Unhurriedly he bent his head and kissed her open mouth and for an instant she felt the burning of his lips, and the shock rippled through her body like the rush and retreat of the tide. Before she could gather her wits for any kind of a coherent remark, her two visitors were pulling on their boots and with a final mocking salute from Garth, they were gone.

Vicki stood where she was in the kitchen, wondering what in the world she was letting herself in for. She had come to the north shore for solitude and peace—so why had she agreed to look after Stephen? To live in the same house with the disturbing Garth Travis? She must be mad! Out of her mind. A year ago she had vowed never to let herself get involved with anyone again—and now, because of a small boy's wistful grey eyes and a man's forceful personality, she was acting as though that vow had never existed. For the first time since Stephen's arrival, some cold hard facts intruded themselves: she could not stay indefinitely at Seal Cove as 'the housekeeper', for the longer she stayed, the more dependent upon her Stephen would get—and maybe the reverse would be true, too, she thought with painful honesty, because already the little boy had insinuated his way into her heart and it was possible that her need of him was a great as his need of her. How would she ever be able to leave? She would be trapped, unable to escape, just as she had been trapped in her marriage ... panic-stricken, she stood rooted to the floor, and if Garth had walked in the door she would have braved his wrath and told him she was not coming. But, of course, he had gone and she wouldn't see him again until he came for her tomorrow. . . .

By midday she and Nils had transferred her chickens to his shed, and he was preparing lunch for her; he had already been out to his traps at dawn. He had been very quiet since she had arrived and told him her plans, but now, as he put a huge plate of ham and eggs in front of her, he said heavily, 'Vicki, maybe it's none of my business, but why are you going to Seal Cove?'

Rather more slowly than was necessary she buttered a piece of bread, knowing he was only asking the same question she had been asking herself. Looking up, she saw puzzlement in the sea-blue eyes, and something else which only belatedly did she recognise as hurt, so that she knew she could tell him nothing less than the truth. 'I lay awake half the night wondering the same thing, Nils, and I don't know if I'm any nearer the answer. There's something about Stephen—he needs me. Perhaps that's it.'

'Maybe I need you, too.'

Her knife clattered against the plate. 'He's just a child, Nils. A child growing up without a mother.'

'You plan to be his mother?' The question spoken with unusual sharpness for Nils.

'Of course I can't be his mother. But I can look after him, do some of the things a real mother does.'

'And what about Garth Travis?'

'What about him?' she said, hearing the note of defensiveness in her voice but unable to prevent it. As an attempt to distract Nils, she added, 'Oh, guess what? Garth is a writer—his pen-name is Paul Tarrant. I loaned you one of his books a while ago—remember?'

'Yes, I do. So Garth is Paul Tarrant. . . .' He rubbed

his beard thoughtfully and lowered his voice. 'There was some kind of fuss about him in the papers a year or more ago—wish I could remember what it was about. Whatever it was, I've forgotten it.' He looked unusually troubled for Nils and for a moment Vicki felt a qualm of foreboding.

'Just make sure you never tell him that I try to write—I'd be embarrassed to show him anything of mine!'

'Your stuff's fine,' Nils said soberly. 'You don't need to apologise for it to anyone.' He cut some more bread. 'But you still haven't answered my question, Vicki—where does Garth Travis fit in this arrangement?'

'He doesn't.'

'Come off it, Vic. The guy's Stephen's father—he lives in the same house.'

'He'll be my employer, that's all.'

Nils poured himself more coffee, his blunt, work-roughened fingers unaccustomedly clumsy, so that some of the hot brown liquid spilled on the table. 'I wish you wouldn't go,' he said abruptly.

'Why, Nils?'

She could see him struggling with his native inarticulateness. 'Don't get me wrong. I like Garth. But he spells trouble—there's a hell of lot more to him than meets the eye, and I don't want you running foul of him.'

'Nils, I won't,' she said, briefly resting her hand on his wrist. 'He's nothing to me—he's just Stephen's father, that's all.' For her own sake she had to believe this—had to forget Garth's ruthless determination, his uncanny perception, the pull of his masculinity.

'That's not all.' Nils stared down at his coffee mug and she could see the dull patches of colour in his wind-burned cheeks. 'I'll miss you, Vicki.'

She knew what it must have cost him to make that admission and felt a rush of affection for him. Dear Nils, as dependable as the tides, as sturdy as the timbers of his own boat. 'It's sweet of you to say that, Nils,' she said softly.

'I know you had a lousy marriage and that's kind of put you off men, but I'd sure like it if some time you'd see your way clear to marrying me.'

Whatever she had expected, it was not this. Unable to think of a thing to say, she watched as he shoved his chair back and grabbed a couple of logs from the woodbox, throwing them in the stove with rather a lot of unnecessary noise —noise that incidentally drowned out the sound of an approaching car. The cast iron door of the stove slammed shut. He wiped his hands down the sides of his pants, looking anywhere but at the silent girl at the table. 'Forget I said it—I know I'm not anywhere good enough for you.'

Swiftly she got to her feet and walked over to him, seizing his hands in hers. 'Don't say that! You're a fine man, Nils, and you've been such a good friend since I moved here. I don't know how I'd have managed without your help that first month.'

He grinned at her with something approaching his normal, uncomplicated manner. 'Took a while to teach you which end of an axe was which, didn't it?'

She giggled. 'Don't exaggerate—it wasn't that bad. I told you my uncle always split the wood while I was growing up.'

At the window a dark head appeared, but neither of them saw it. 'I'm not going that far away, Nils,' Vicki said persuasively. 'I hope you'll come and visit me?'

'Yeah. . . .' Visibly he steeled himself. 'I meant what I said about marrying you.'

Briefly she rested her forehead on his shoulder. When she looked up, her eyes were misty with tears. 'Dear Nils,' she said unsteadily. 'I'm truly honoured that you asked me—and if I were to marry anyone right now it would be you. I—I really trust you.' She smiled wryly. 'And that's no small admission for me to make! But you must know I can't do it. It's nothing personal against you. I just don't think I'll ever get married again.'

Awkwardly he put his arms around her. She felt none of the panic she had felt in Garth's arms, but equally none of the piercing sweetness; she simply felt comfortable and at home, as though a brother was holding her. She heard him say gruffly, 'Okay. I never really expected you to say yes. But will you promise to keep in touch with me?'

'I promise,' she said solemnly. And because she was genuinely moved, she leaned forward and kissed him, by the touch of her lips trying to express her gratitude.

From outside came the rattle of footsteps on the stones and the sharp rat-tat of knuckles against the door. She and Nils sprang apart, Vicki hastily smoothing her hair as Nils went to the door . . . it must be Garth, she knew. Had he seen them?

'Hi, Nils,' she heard Garth say. 'Vicki here? I went up to the house and it was all locked up.'

'Sure, come on in,' Nils muttered with none of Garth's self-possession.

Garth stepped in the door, a single glance encompassing the girl's flushed cheeks. 'I hope I wasn't interrupting anything?' he said smoothly.

Nils's skin reddened under his tan. 'No—of course not,' he stammered. 'We were just finishing lunch, weren't we, Vic?' Not waiting for her to reply, he rushed on, 'Want a coffee?'

'No, thanks—if Vicki's ready, we'd better get going. I want to be back before Stephen gets home from school.'

'My cases are over there,' Vicki said coolly, picking up her jacket from the bunk.

Nils stood in stoic silence as she put on her gold parka and perched a fleecy white tam on her dark hair; perhaps it was something in the younger man's demeanour that caused Garth to say abruptly, 'Nils, feel free to come and visit Vicki any time you can. I'm in the phone book.'

'Okay—thanks,' Nils said gruffly.

'I'll put your suitcases in the car, Vicki.' With the slightest edge to his voice Garth added, 'Don't be long. Goodbye, Nils.'

As soon as he had gone, Vicki said quickly, 'Take care of yourself, won't you, Nils, and be sure and come for a visit.' Wanting to remove that look of baffled misery from his face, she added, 'You remember the carving you gave me? It's in my case and I'll put it in my room so I'll have it to remind me of you.'

Sudden hope flared in his eyes and she wondered if she had done the right thing. But it was too late now. 'I must go—'bye.'

She had already turned to leave when he swung her around and pulled her to him, his kiss as clumsy as it was fierce, and sheer surprise held her motionless. 'There,' he said breathlessly, looking faintly amazed at his own daring, 'I'm just staking my claim. Be careful, won't you, Vic? I'm not sure I trust that guy.'

Neither was she, but she was not about to tell Nils that. 'I will.' A quick wave of her hand and she escaped, running up the slope to Garth's car.

CHAPTER SIX

GARTH leaned over and opened the door for her. 'I hope I didn't rush you,' he said sarcastically.

Recklessly Vicki took up the challenge. 'Not at all.'

'Just what *did* I interrupt when I arrived?'

'What gives you the idea you interrupted anything?'

'Perhaps I should confess that I was watching at the window.'

'Oh.' She was silent for a moment in utter consternation before she felt the healthy pricking of anger. 'Do you make a habit of spying on people?'

'I'm rarely interested enough to do so,' he drawled.

'I suppose I should feel flattered.'

'I'm not sure flattered is the word I'd use—what's up with you and Nils, Vicki?'

She could not be bothered to prevaricate—and besides, she was fairly sure he would get the truth out of her sooner or later. 'He was asking me to marry him.'

'And what did you say? It could hardly be yes, or you wouldn't be here.'

'I told him if I were to marry anyone it would be him,' she snapped, irritated. 'I also told him I was never going to get married again.'

'How very confusing,' he said silkily, steering the car around a sharp curve.

'Stop making fun of me, Garth!'

He dropped his taunting manner of speech and said flatly, 'Not only confusing but untrue.'

'I wouldn't lie to Nils,' she said hotly.

'You *are* going to get married again, Vicki—to me.'

His attention appeared to be totally on the road, and in a simmering silence she stared at his profile—straight nose, uncompromising chin, firm set of lips. 'Garth,' she pleaded, 'I do wish you'd stop this—I don't find it amusing.'

He flicked her a quick glance, seeing the troubled brown eyes and soft, uncertain mouth. 'I wouldn't want you to think I'm joking,' he said calmly. 'Because I'm not—I mean every word of it. I'm not trying to tease you, or upset you. I'm simply telling you my intentions.'

She felt as though she was struggling in quicksand, with no firm foothold to support her. 'This is a crazy conversation,' she said, her voice shaking a little. 'You must know I'm not going to marry you, Garth—why on earth should I?'

'Any number of reasons. I'm rich and I'm famous——'

'Oh, don't!' she cried. 'You know that's not what I meant.'

'Just be quiet and listen for a minute,' he countered, his intonation pure granite. 'Don't knock the fact that I've got money—you haven't said much, but I would gather you're far from well off. Money, handled correctly, is a damned useful commodity.'

'Handled correctly is right,' she said bitterly, re-membering how Barry had squandered her money, as recklessly extravagant as if it would go on for ever. Which, of course, it hadn't.

'Why do you say that, Vicki?'

'Never mind.' It had hurt her too much, been too humiliating—how could she share it?

'Some day—soon—you're going to tell me the truth about your marriage.'

'I've never told anyone that, and I'm not likely to start with you,' she said rudely.

'That's the trouble—you've kept it locked up inside you and it's festering there, poisoning your whole outlook.'

'Do stop analysing me!'

'Came too close to the truth for comfort, didn't I?'

She was silent, staring down at the tightly clenched fingers in her lap, and after an instant's pause Garth went on imperturbably, 'To continue the catalogue of my virtues—I'm famous. I'm lucky enough to have found something I like doing and I do it well—writing. So that's that. I've been told I'm not unattractive to the female of

the species. I don't smoke, I don't gamble, I rarely drink
to excess. And I have all my own teeth.'

She glared at him in total frustration. 'I never know
when you're joking or when you're serious!'

After a quick glance behind him in the mirror, he
pulled the car over to the side of the road, where there
was a gravelled look-off beside the ocean. 'Get out,' he
said unceremoniously.

The wind pierced her clothing as she walked over to
the shore. Twenty feet below, the cold, surly waters of the
Atlantic hurled themselves at the rocks, breaking up into
pellets of spray that were flung high in the air only to fall
back into the seething foam. Garth had joined her and
with one hand turned her to face him. 'About marrying
you, I'm completely serious,' he said, raising his voice to
be heard above the sea's constant brawl.

'You have yet to give me one good reason why I should
think you *are* serious.' With sudden violence she added, 'I
don't give a damn about your money or your fame!'

He said slowly, 'I don't believe you do, do you?' Quite
suddenly there was nothing in his face but simple liking
for her, and his smile was lit with a rare warmth that
penetrated all her defences much as, earlier, Stephen's
smile had done the same thing. He went on, 'You don't
know how good it is to hear that—one of the penalties of
fame is that one's never sure when one is being liked for
oneself.'

It seemed the most natural thing in the world that he
should lean forward and kiss her. His lips were cold and
tasted salty, yet they took the chill from her bones and
the ache from her heart. Unconsciously she swayed towards him. With one hand he pulled the knitted cap from
her head and as the wind seized her hair, whipping it
around her face, his kiss deepened and his arms held her
close.

For Vicki, reality was suspended. She forgot that she
hated to be touched, for his arms represented warmth
and comfort and healing. His hands moulded her to the
hard length of his body and her own hands pulled his

head closer, her fingers entangled in his hair. Miraculously there was nothing in the world but the glory of his kiss, and that kiss became everything she had ever wanted or desired. . . .

When he finally released her, her eyes were dazed, drowned in a sea of new emotions that had welled up from the hidden depths of her being. Garth stared at her, in his own eyes a question that gradually hardened into conviction. 'You told me you were married and I have to believe you,' he said. 'But I'd be willing to swear that's the first time you've ever been kissed like that. . . .'

She pulled away from him, her face as shocked as if he had physically struck her. Oh, God, what had she done? she thought incoherently. A smile, a kiss, and she had betrayed herself. 'Your lawyer friend looked it up in the registry,' she said. 'You know I was married.'

'Yes . . . but what kind of a marriage was it?'

He, of all people, must never know the truth. 'I was Barry's wife for over a year,' she said evasively.

'His wife in every sense of the word?'

She stared straight into his eyes, her heart beating frantically. 'Yes—of course.'

Garth made a sudden sharp gesture of frustration. 'Maybe I was wrong, then . . . but you know, Vicki, I've just given you another good reason for us to marry.'

'What do you mean?' She shoved her cold-numbed hands into her pockets.

'Sex,' he said bluntly. 'I want you. And, when you let yourself forget all your inhibitions, you want me.'

She shook her head in mute denial, trying to forget those fleeting moments when every facet of her being had melted into a passionate longing to be kissed and held. 'No,' she whispered. 'No, Garth. That's the very worst of reasons to get married——'

'Give me a better one, then!'

Beleaguered, she said the first thing that came into her head. 'What about love? You've never mentioned the word.'

It was his turn to react. She saw his tall frame shudder.

As if he could not face her any longer, he turned his head towards the horizon, looking out over the ocean's cold grey wastes.

'Garth?' she said tentatively. 'What have I said?'

Still not looking at her, he said tonelessly, 'I married once for love, Vicki—I won't do it again.'

His own honesty seemed to demand an equal honesty from her. Besides, she wanted to remove that haunted look from his face—although why, she could not have said. 'So did I,' she said steadily.

He dragged his eyes away from the restless, churning sea. With an attempt at humour that did not quite succeed, he said wryly, 'So I guess we can remove that from our list of reasons.' She shivered, hunching her shoulders against the wind's bite, not knowing what to say. It was he who spoke. 'You're cold—let's go back to the car.'

This time when he swung back on to the road, he drove in silence, his features with a remoteness that she dared not disturb. He handled the car with consummate skill, hugging the curves, revving up on the straight stretches, and despite their speed, Vicki felt perfectly safe, sensing that he would take no unnecessary risks. Her thoughts were free to wander, and as her eyes idly followed the cliffs and shoals of the shoreline, she pondered the conversation they had just had. It was not the first time Garth had announced his intention of marrying her, and deep in her heart she knew he wasn't joking—for reasons of his own, he wanted her to be his wife. He did not love her any more than she loved him, and in fact she was more than ever convinced that he still loved his dead wife. . . . Perhaps all he wanted was a surrogate mother for Stephen—and a woman in his bed. She would look after Stephen to the best of her ability; but for the rest, she concluded decisively, Garth Travis would have to look elsewhere. There must be any number of women who would jump at the chance of marrying him—certainly of sharing his bed, she thought with unwonted cynicism, remembering only too clearly the latent strength of his embrace and the probing sweetness of his kiss. Nothing that Barry had ever done had caused her to so lose herself—to forget time and place, reason and common sense.

She leaned back in her seat, which cushioned her luxuriously, and her eyes closed.

A voice pulled her back from a confused dream of mist and crows and a man's grey eyes. 'Vicki, we're nearly there. Wake up!'

She rubbed her eyes, stifling a yawn. 'Sorry, I didn't mean to fall asleep. Goodness! Where are we?'

'A mile or so from Seal Cove—didn't I warn you that I lived in the back of beyond?'

'I don't recall that you did,' she answered absently, surveying the wild beauty of their surroundings with keen interest. They were driving along a narrow dirt road, more nearly a track than a road, which wound precariously along the edge of the cliffs. To her right there was the vast expanse of the ocean, empty, seemingly void of life, its gaunt cliffs edged with foam as white as a seagull's breast. To her left were the rounded hills of the highlands, overgrown with tough, wiry spruce trees and stunted shrubs, traversed by brooks whose crystal-clear waters tumbled their way to the sea. Deep snow lay in the hollows. From above came the peevish cry of a solitary gull, while over everything hung the brooding immensity of the cloud-filled sky.

'I've never been this far north before,' said Vicki, marvelling. 'It's magnificent—but it makes me feel very insignificant.'

'Exactly—it puts us and all our little schemes and emotions in their proper place, doesn't it?' said Garth with a bitterness she could not understand.

'Perhaps,' she said doubtfully. Half joking, half serious, she went on, 'But I think it calls for the grand emotions rather than the petty, don't you? For passion and tragedy and deathless love. . . .' Abruptly she fell silent, wishing she had not spoken.

So suddenly that she was jerked forward in her seat, he braked the car. 'So you feel that, too.' He looked her full in the face and there was the glitter of reckless triumph in his eyes. 'I knew I was right—there's more to you than meets the eye, isn't there, Vicki Peters?'

'That's surely true of most people,' she said carefully.

'You more so than others. You with your coolness and your control and your lack of involvement—it's all a façade. Underneath you're a passionate woman, vibrant and sensitive. I'm going to bring you to life, Vicki. I'm going to release you from the prison you've built for yourself——'

She had to stop him. 'Did it occur to you I might be happy as I am?'

'Happy? You don't know the meaning of the word.'

'You're so incredibly arrogant!' she cried. 'You've known me less than a month and you think you have the right to sit there and dictate to me how I should behave and what I should be feeling. Just who the *hell* do you think you are?'

His eyes lingered appreciatively on the gold sparks in her eyes and the flush of anger in her cheeks and before she could move he clamped his hands around her head and began to kiss her. His lips were hard and rough, giving no quarter, demanding from her an equal intensity, an equal lack of pretence.

She fought him every inch of the way, trying desperately to maintain the very coolness and control of which he had accused her. But it was impossible. Dry tinder to his flame, she was swept up into the conflagration of a kiss that scorched and burned and devoured her. Then she was in his arms with his hands roaming her body like tongues of fire, his heart thudding against her own like the pulsing of flame. She could not bear for his kiss to continue, for she was being consumed, and equally she could not bear for it to end. . . .

End it did. Garth thrust her away and the triumph was blatant now, blazing in his eyes, beating in all his pulses. 'I can do with you what I will, Vicki,' he said thickly. 'There's no use fighting me. You were meant to be my woman, and that's what you're going to be.'

She stared at him dumbly as the tumult in her body slowly subsided. One last flicker and it was gone, and she was left with only dead, cold ashes. 'No,' she whispered hoarsely. 'No, I won't let you——'

'You can't stop me.'

Scarcely knowing what she was doing, she fumbled for the door handle. 'I want to go home,' she said childishly.

'You are home.' A gesture of his hand encompassed the lonely grandeur of the hills and sea. 'Wherever I am will be your home.'

No, no, no . . . was she speaking the word or was it merely beating in her brain like the throbbing of her blood? 'I can't stay with you, Garth—take me back,' she said, her voice so thin as to be almost unrecognisable.

His hand tightened cruelly on her wrist. 'You promised Stephen. And I'm holding you to that promise.'

'Yes, I promised Stephen! But I promised nothing to you. You must leave me alone, Garth. Please. . . .' Her pride in tatters, her eyes beseeching, she moved her hands in a mute gesture of appeal.

He turned the ignition key and the engine roared back to life. 'No.'

She was caught. Because of Stephen, she could not obey all her instincts, which were screaming at her to get out of the car and run for her life. 'Garth,' she said, trying to sound as convincing as she could, 'I don't want to let Stephen down. But if you persist in—in harassing me like this, I shall have no choice.' She raised her chin defiantly. 'I shall have to leave. Is that clear?'

He said lazily, 'Just around this corner you'll get the first view of the house.'

'Oh! Didn't you hear a word I said?'

'I heard you, Vicki . . . there. What do you think of it?'

The track was winding down a steep hill to a sheltered cove with a narrow strip of beach and a creosoted wharf. A white-painted Cape Islander swayed gently on the swell. Behind the beach were granite cliffs and an open field, holding back the forest's encroachment. But the house was not safely tucked among the shelter of the trees.

Instead it had been built on the very summit of the cliffs, where it challenged the harsh contours of the land. It was constructed of naturally weathered boards, their soft grey sheen as much a part of the surroundings as the rocks and trees. Its roof was all angles and inclines while great sheets of glass overlooked the ocean, and a sundeck jutted out almost to the cliff's edge.

As she gazed at it, Vicki felt she had learned more about Garth Travis in the past few moments than she had learned since they had met. Defiance, yes . . . the house expressed that. But more powerfully it expressed an attempt at integration with a harsh and unforgiving environment: Garth knew the cruelty of life, yet could wreak from it a harmony and a beauty. . . . She gave a tiny sigh. 'I've never seen a house so beautifully attuned to its surroundings. The architect must have been a genius.'

He gave a deprecating laugh. 'Well, I designed a fair bit of it myself—although I had to get an architect to transfer my ideas to blueprints, of course. I'm glad you like it.'

'Like' was too mild a word for the effect the house had had on her, but she did not feel like sharing that with him. All she said was, 'I'm looking forward to seeing the inside.'

After Garth had parked the car, they entered by the side door and as they walked down a long vaulted hallway he said, 'Let's put your cases in your room and then I'll show you the rest of the house. You're next to me and across the hall from Stephen—I thought you'd like to hear the sound of the ocean.' He pushed open a door and she preceded him into the room.

Tall glass panels comprised one entire wall, with sheer white drapes pulled back so that the magnificent view of cliffs and sea became as much a part of the room as the bone white carpet that lay on the dark oak floor, and the stone fireplace. Had that been all, the room would have been austere, even cold. But the double bed was covered with a quilted spread of a rich rose hue, and the chairs by the hearth had been upholstered in a figured cream and rose brocade; the colours glowed like jewels.

'Bathroom through here,' Garth said prosaically. 'Lots of cupboard space. Bookshelves and a desk in the alcove. Do you think you'll be comfortable?'

'How could I fail to be?' Vicki breathed, her eyes slowly taking in every detail of the room, her lips curving with delight. 'It's the most beautiful room I've ever had.'

'Good. Come on and I'll show you——'

A door slammed and there was the sound of running footsteps. 'Dad! Did Vicki come?'

'She's in here.'

Stephen hurtled into the room. 'Hi, Vicki! I brought some friends home to meet you.' He grabbed her hand. 'They're waiting outside.'

Laughing, Vicki let herself be led through the kitchen to the back door and was solemnly introduced to two small boys, Tony and Andrew Hunter, both identically clad in nylon parkas and knitted caps, both with mops of the most vivid red hair she had ever seen. 'Their parents live half a mile farther up the road,' Garth interposed. 'I'm sure Carole will be over to meet you tomorrow.'

As all three boys seemed to be eyeing her expectantly, Vicki said in sudden inspiration, 'Is there any popping corn?' Stephen found some in the back of one of the cupboards and with his help Vicki soon had bowls of fluffy buttered popcorn in front of each of them, together with glasses of chocolate milk. The kitchen seemed to be full of warmth and chatter, and suddenly she was supremely happy, all her doubts and anxieties dissipated in the certainty that here was where she belonged. Stephen said something to her and she made a laughing retort, quite unaware that from his stance by the sink Garth was watching her, his eyes inscrutable, his fingers methodically shredding to pieces the empty packet of popcorn.

The rest of the day passed by in a whirl of activity; there was supper to prepare in the unfamiliar kitchen, and Stephen's homework and bath to supervise. Then, as part of what was obviously a regular routine, Garth read a bedtime story while, at Stephen's request, Vicki perched on the end of the little boy's bed; the story was about galleons and pirates and Spanish gold and seemed decidedly bloodthirsty to Vicki, although as the final villain walked the plank, Stephen's eyelids were drooping. ''Night Vicki,' he said sleepily. ''Night, Dad.' He wound his arms around his father's neck, his fingers very small against the broad expanse of Garth's back, and Vicki felt her throat tighten with emotion—there could be no doubt of the love between father and son, and equally no doubt that Garth took the obligation of fatherhood very seriously.

Barry had never wanted children, and with sudden clarity Vicki recognised how totally he had lacked Garth's solidity, his sense of responsibility, his ability to maintain a lasting relationship. Unromantic-sounding traits, she supposed, but far more real, far more dependable, than all Barry's charm and fickle enthusiasms.

Someone shook her shoulder and she blinked, for she had been a long way away from Stephen's cheerful bedroom with its bright red carpet and colourful wallpaper. She got up and left the room with Garth, his hand still on her shoulder, and out in the hallway he turned her to face him. 'I'll give you a hand with the dishes,' he said quietly. 'You look bushed.'

She was still grappling with her revelation and as she raised her brown eyes there was perplexity in their depths. 'I'm all right,' she said absently. 'You don't have to bother.'

'It's no bother—I'd like to help.'

Her mind still elsewhere, she added abruptly, 'You're a good father.'

He frowned. 'What brought that on?'

'Oh, just watching you and Stephen together.' Her voice was wistful. 'He's a lucky little boy.'

'You never had a child?' he asked gently.

'No.' The word was bitten off and he must have felt the sudden tension in her shoulder. Defensively, 'I was only married for a year.'

He steered her down the hall towards the kitchen and

only later did she realise he might not have wanted Stephen to hear their conversation. 'But you wanted children?' Vicki nodded unhappily. 'You'd be a good mother, I'm sure.'

She smiled faintly. 'Thank you. I'll certainly do my best with Stephen.'

'I know you will.' Through the thin cotton of her shirt she felt his fingers tighten on her arm. 'We've just found another reason for you to marry me. . . .' For a moment she gazed at him uncomprehendingly. 'You could have a child, Vicki—our child. A brother or a sister for Stephen. . . .'

Shock drove the colour from her face. She tried to pull away from him, but his fingers were still clamped on her shoulder. There was a tiny sound of tearing fabric as the top button of her shirt was ripped off and the neckline fell open. She didn't even notice. 'You're crazy!' she whispered raggedly. 'I couldn't do that——'

'Why not?' he said levelly.

'Because . . . because—it all sounds so cold-blooded!' she said wildly. 'Like one of those arranged marriages. People don't do that kind of thing nowadays.'

'There's no reason in the world why we couldn't do it.' Deliberately he let his hands slide down her arms to the curve of her waist and his eyes lingered on the creamy skin of her throat and the shadowed hollow between her breasts. 'I would like to give you a child, Vicki.'

Her cheeks flamed with colour, although the very quietness of his voice mesmerised her such that she was unable to move. Helplessly she closed her eyes as she was flooded with longings as old as time—to feel her body quicken with his child, to bear within her a life they had both created, to hold his son or daughter in her arms . . . Garth's child.

Then she felt his face against her hair and the warmth of his lips travel down her cheek to her mouth. His hands drew her waist to his hips and it was almost a reflex action that caused her to slide her arms around him. It was a kiss that seemed to go on for ever. Her hands clutched his shirt, for had he released her she would have fallen. But the only release was when his lips left her mouth and explored the slenderness of her neck, the hollowed throat, and then the softness of one breast. His hand left her waist to cup her flesh, pulling aside the lacy fabric of her bra, and as she felt the imprint of his tongue she almost yielded to the aching surge of passion that seized her as inexorably as would the mighty waves of the sea, to drown her in their depths.

Something held her back. A deep-held fear of surrender? A fleeting remembrance of the triumph in his eyes? She never knew. But suddenly she was fighting him, pulling back, her voice thin with fear as she begged him to let go. Had he chosen not to, she would have been totally at his mercy; however, for reasons of his own, he released her immediately, stepping back, his arms falling to his sides. Not until he spoke did she realise he was formidably angry. 'Still running, Vicki? Still playing the coward?'

An answering anger burst into flame, fuelled by the remnants of a desire more devastating than anything she had ever experienced. 'So I'm a coward because I won't jump into bed with you the minute you touch me! What kind of values do you have? You know damn well if I did, you'd label me cheap, easy, all those ugly words men use——'

'Be quiet! I hate those words as much as you do! No, Vicki, you're a coward because you won't trust your emotions and your responses—you're fighting them all the way. When I marry you, you can be sure it won't be one of those separate bedroom arrangements—I'm not that kind of a man. You'll share my bed just as you shared Barry's—so stop acting like a terrified virgin!'

She swallowed an upwelling of hysterical laughter with an effort that left her weak. 'Unfortunately I am still declining your offer of marriage—and certainly your offer of anything else,' she said coldly, the effect rather spoiled by the tremor in her voice. 'Now if you'll excuse me, I'd like to get the kitchen cleaned up so I can unpack and go to bed—I'm very tired.'

'No headache?' he said sarcastically. 'That's the classic female excuse, you know.'

'I don't need excuses!' she flared. 'I'm not married to you——'

'Not yet.' There was a subtle threat in the two quietly spoken words, and she backed away, picking up a couple of used plates and carrying them over to the stainless steel sink. As if he had suddenly lost interest in her, Garth snapped, 'Leave those—I'll clean up.'

'No, I——'

'Vicki, it's only a matter of loading the dishwasher and I'm perfectly capable of that. Go to bed. You'll have to be up at seven if you want to get Stephen off to school.' With a curt nod of dismissal he turned his back on her and began rinsing off the plates.

Subduing a very childish urge to pull a rude face at him, Vicki turned on her heel and stalked off to her room, closing the door as sharply as she could without actually slamming it. Infuriating man! She'd never met anyone so sure of himself; deep down she was certain Garth did not doubt her eventual surrender. His technique was rather like that of erosion, she thought ruefully, of water gradually wearing away the stone . . . one of these days she'd say yes simply to keep him quiet.

She went over to the window to pull the curtains. It was completely dark, and in the cloudless sky the stars twinkled like tiny diamonds flung across a black velvet cloth; she could hear the regular fall and retreat of the waves on the beach, while from the headland far to the right a beacon flickered on and off . . . on and off.

Earlier in the day she had told Garth that these surroundings should elicit nothing petty, and now as she leaned her forehead against the cold glass, she knew that for some reason he had the power to arouse in her an intensity of feeling that was new to her. Whatever the emotion he evoked—anger, desire, joy—she was consumed by it, and somehow this frightened her more than anything else he could say or do; it was as though a new Vicki was emerging, a woman she had not known existed, a creature of fire and passion whom, she was sure, neither her relatives nor Barry would have recognised. There had been no place for emotion in the long dreary years with her aunt and uncle; laughter had been looked upon askance, pleasure as a sin. As for Barry, the last thing he had been interested in was his young bride's feelings, and very quickly she had learned to hide them behind a brittle mask of poise and self-control, burying any remnants of generosity and love.

What was it about Garth that caused her to be different when she was with him? More alive, more of a woman. Moving away from the window she undressed for bed and for a moment stood naked in front of the full-length mirror on the cupboard door. Knowing that Garth wanted her, that he found her beautiful, she was able to recognise the intrinsic seductiveness of the firm pink-tipped breasts and of the curve and flow of waist, hip and thigh. Suddenly shy, she grabbed her nightdress and pulled it over her head, then got into bed. She had left the curtains open so she could watch the illimitable darkness and listen to the ceaseless rhythm of the waves, repetitive and soothing. Within minutes she was asleep.

CHAPTER SEVEN

Vicki awoke to dazzling sunlight and a small boy in pyjamas bouncing on the end of her bed. 'Wake up! It's breakfast time. Are you going to make a chocolate cake today?'

She sat up, reaching for her dressing gown just as Garth walked in the door balancing a cup of tea on a tray. Unfortunately she was not wearing the voluminous nightgown he had seen her in before; this one was pale pink nylon, lace-edged and low-cut. 'Pass me my dressing gown, Stephen, please,' she said, trying to look anywhere but at Garth.

'Are you going to bring her tea every morning, Dad?'

'It's bribery,' Garth said cheerfully, 'so she'll get our breakfast.'

He passed Vicki the tray and as she took it she caught the tang of his aftershave lotion; his hair was still damp from the shower, although he was fully dressed in lean-fitting cords and an open-necked shirt. She took a sip of tea, her eyelashes fluttering down so she would not have to look at him. 'I must get up,' she said. 'You have to have a lunch packed for school, don't you, Stephen?'

'I'll look after that until you get used to the routine,' Garth offered. 'Come on, Steve, we'd better get out of here so Vicki can get up.' As Stephen ran across the hall, Garth paused in the doorway to say softly, 'I'm glad to see you're as beautiful first thing in the morning as last thing at night. Not that I was really worrying. . . .'

The sun was gleaming in his dark hair, highlighting the strong bones of his face and the masculine outlines of his long, lean body. She could remember only too clearly the hard imprint of that body on hers and the bruising strength of his arms. As if he could read her mind, he let his eyes wander suggestively over the soft swell of her breasts under the filmy nylon.

Vicki could feel the heat rising in her face. 'Shut the door on your way out, please,' she said, striving for dignity but sounding merely peevish. He did as she asked and she leapt out of bed, thinking of all the things she wanted to accomplish today in an effort to drive the memory of that mocking regard from her mind.

Breakfast on the table. Lunch packed. A final wave goodbye as Stephen ran up to the road to catch the school bus. Under the bustle of activity Vicki had found time to wonder what would happen once she and Garth were alone in the house. She was soon to find out. Garth poured himself a second mug of coffee from the percolator and said crisply, 'I work until noon in the study, Vicki. If you can find time to make lunch, soup and a sandwich will do—if not, I'll get my own. After lunch I go out for a while, then I work until supper time.'

She must have looked surprised, because he added drily, 'Did you think I wandered around the house, waiting for inspiration to hit? Writing is ten per cent inspiration and ninety per cent hard work—and I'd better emphasise right now that if I'm in the study with the door closed, I'm only to be disturbed if the house is burning down around my ears, or if something happens to Stephen. Not for anything else. Is that clear?'

She nodded meekly, aware of a curious mixture of relief and disappointment as he left the room. Shrugging off her feelings, she decided to begin by cleaning up the breakfast dishes. The kitchen, like the rest of the house, represented a very clever blend of the useful and the decorative; it had every possible convenience, yet its pine cupboards, hanging plants, and brass ornaments saved it from being merely functional. She was hard at work going through all the cupboards so she would know where to find things, when there came a tap at the door and a cheerful female voice called, 'Anyone home?'

Vicki stood up, a half-smile already on her lips as she saw the visitor's flaming head of hair—it could be no one but Carole Hunter, Tony and Andrew's mother. 'Hello,' she said. 'I'm Vicki Peters—you must be Mrs Hunter.'

'Well!' Carole exclaimed, stopping dead in her tracks, 'Well, well . . . so you're Vicki. Aren't boys hopeless? From Tony's description I thought you were plump and fortyish. You don't look a day over twenty-one—am I right?' Vicki gave a bemused nod. 'And you're absolutely gorgeous!' Carole grinned engagingly. 'I hope you don't mind me saying so. Philip—he's my husband—always says I talk first and think afterwards. You don't mind, do you? Can I come in?'

Vicki finally found her tongue. 'Of course—please do. Here, sit down.' For Carole, she now saw, was at least eight months pregnant, carrying herself with an unconscious pride that was somehow very touching.

'Thanks. Phew!—I walked over, because I'm supposed to get as much exercise as I can, the doctor says. Only three weeks to go. I've had two miscarriages since Andrew was born, so I'm trying to do everything I should and nothing I shouldn't. We really hope it's a girl—I've been knitting little pink things ever since I found out I was pregnant. Nothing blue at all. Do you think that'll work?'

Vicki laughed. 'Well, I certainly hope so,' she said diplomatically. 'Is a cup of tea on your list of shoulds?'

'Yes, thank goodness. Now tell me about yourself, Vicki. We heard how you rescued Stephen—so I know how brave you are. What sign are you?'

'Sign?' said Vicki, bewildered by Carole's somewhat haphazard means of conversation.

'You know—astrology. Horoscopes.'

'Oh, Taurus, I think.'

'Really? When's your birthday?'

'Two weeks from today, actually.'

'Garth is Leo. So that means you're very compatible.'

'Don't you start, too!' As soon as she had spoken, Vicki could have bitten off her tongue. Making as much noise as she could, she got out cups and saucers and poured milk into a jug.

Fortunately, however, Carole misinterpreted her statement. 'I suppose Stephen wants to make you a permanent fixture, does he?'

'I have to pass the acid test today and make chocolate cake—a lot will depend on that!' Vicki said lightly.

Carole laughed. 'Well, I think they're both very fortunate to have you. Stephen needs a woman around—and who knows, maybe Garth does too. Will you have enough here to keep you busy, though? Because Mrs Sampson from up the road does all the cleaning and washing and so on, doesn't she?'

'Garth mentioned something like that.'

'You'll have to find a hobby of some kind. There's not much entertainment at Seal Cove—you have to make your own.'

Because already she liked Carole very much, Vicki said shyly, 'Well, actually, I have a project on the go—a children's book that I'm writing and illustrating myself.'

'Really? Two writers in one house—I'm impressed!'

'Oh, Garth doesn't know,' Vicki said hastily. 'I wouldn't want him to see it.'

'Why ever not?'

'Carole, he's famous—and this is the first book I've ever tried.'

'Do you think he didn't have a first book? Of course he did. Everyone has to start somewhere.'

Vicki was only half convinced. 'I suppose you're right . . . milk and sugar?'

'No sugar—trying to cut down.'

The talk subsided into a comfortable discussion of diets, recipes, and the latest fashions, until Carole finally got up. 'I'd better head back—I don't exactly break any speed records these days! Come and visit me, Vicki—I'd love you to.'

'I will—thanks.' From the door Vicki waved goodbye, pleased to know that she had made a new friend.

With surprising ease, Vicki's days fell into a routine. Her only responsibilities were to cook the meals and look after Stephen, and neither of these were onerous duties, particularly since the initial rapport between her and Stephen was deepening as the days went by, and already she had forgotten that the first two weeks were supposed to be a trial period. She saw surprisingly little of Garth; from what he had told her, she knew he was working on a new novel, and every evening after Stephen went to bed he would shut himself in the study again and she would hear the faint clicking of the typewriter keys. He made no demands on her, treating her with a distant friendliness that sometimes made her wonder if she had dreamed his talk of marriage; she had asked to come as the house-keeper, she thought wryly, so she shouldn't be complain-ing when she was treated as such. However, as the days passed, his manner piqued her more than a little. Luckily she had Stephen to distract her, as well as frequent—and always entertaining—visits with Carole, besides work on her own book. For Carole had been right—there was spare time, and often in the afternoons while a pie was in the oven or a stew simmering on the stove, Vicki would spread her papers on the kitchen table and immerse herself in a story that was becoming increasingly more real to her. So it was that when Garth came unexpectedly into the kitchen one afternoon, he had to speak to her twice before she heard him.

'What are you doing?' he demanded.

She blushed, looking the picture of guilt as she shuffled the neatly written pages into a pile. 'Oh—nothing.'

'Come off it, Vicki—I asked you a question.'

She said crossly, 'I'm trying to write a book—a chil-dren's book.'

His mouth tightened ominously. 'Carole had mentioned something of the sort to me, but I'd decided she must have got it wrong—I couldn't imagine why you wouldn't have told me about it.'

'Stop glowering at me as if I'm a criminal or some-thing!'

'Not a criminal—just a normally deceptive female.'

Stung, she retorted, 'I'm not!'

His eyes were cynical. 'I suppose that's one of the reasons you came here, is it? Working for Paul Tarrant could be very useful to an aspiring young writer.'

'That's a hateful thing to say, Garth—I'd be the last

person to use you like that!'

'Then why didn't you tell me—couldn't you have trusted me just a little?'

Her temper died as quickly as it had sprung up. She had hurt him, she thought in bewilderment. Abruptly she pushed back her chair and walked over to him, her brown eyes perturbed. 'It wasn't that I didn't trust you, Garth—truly. In fact, you could say it was just the opposite. It's because I do trust your judgment that I was scared to let you see my writing. Because if *you* say it's no good, then I'll know it's not . . . do you understand?'

He nodded slowly. 'Will you let me see it?'

She gulped, gathering her courage. 'Yes.'

'You look as though you're going to your own execution!'

'That's the way I feel.' Before she could change her mind, she picked up the untidy bundle of papers and thrust them at him.

'Thanks—I'll go and read them right now.'

'Oh dear, must you?'

'The reason I came out here in the first place is because I've been stuck on page ninety-one since ten o'clock this morning—so this is just what I need,' he said cheerfully. 'Apple pie for dessert? Good!' And he was gone.

Vicki prepared the evening meal, laid the table, admired Stephen's English test, and talked to the Hunter boys, all with her mind only a quarter on what she was doing. She was just taking the roast out of the oven when Garth walked in, holding her manuscript, his face very serious. Her heart sank. He hadn't liked it—and now, because he wouldn't lie about something so important to her, he was going to have to tell her so. The hot pan was burning her fingers through the oven gloves and hurriedly she put it down, bracing herself for the worst.

'How long have you been writing?' he asked curiously.

'I used to write stories when I was growing up on the farm. But this is my first serious attempt.'

'I see. You're a mysterious creature, Vicki.' He indicated the papers which he had put on the table. 'I feel as though I've just discovered a whole part of you that I didn't know existed—I wonder how many more surprises you have in store for me.'

She could stand the suspense no longer. 'But the book——' she burst out. 'What about the book?'

He raised his eyebrows in surprise. 'That's what I'm trying to tell you. It's good—very good. Interesting characters, excellent dialogue and lots of momentum—and your illustrations are just right. Oh, there are a few things here and there that could be polished up a bit, but the essence of it should remain as it is.'

'You like it?' she said incredulously, sitting down with a thud on the nearest chair. 'You really mean that it's good?'

'I know just the publisher to send it to.'

'You think it could be *published*?'

'Well, of course,' he said impatiently. 'That's why we write, isn't it?'

'Oh, Garth. . . .' She gazed at him, her eyes gold with wonderment, her cheeks flushed.

'Come here a minute.'

Thinking he wanted to show her something on the manuscript she got up and walked around the table, smiling up at him. 'What do you want?'

'This.' His kiss began gently, so that her first instinctive quiver of resistance stilled and died. Because she was happy and excited, all the generosity of her nature, stifled for so many years, came to the surface and she flung her arms around his neck, kissing him back with a fervour that perhaps surprised them both. His arms tightened around her.

There was a thump of footsteps up the back stairs to the kitchen. 'Dad, have you seen my—oh. . . .'

Vicki tried to pull free of Garth's embrace, but his arms remained tightly clasped around her waist and without an undignified struggle it was impossible. She turned her head, her face scarlet, to find three pairs of eyes surveying her with interest and calculation—Stephen, Tony and Andrew.

Going straight to the heart of the matter with all a small boy's directness, Stephen asked hopefully, 'Are you going to marry Vicki, Dad? Mr Hunter kisses Mrs Hunter sometimes, and they're married.'

'I saw Carrie MacIntosh kissing Simon Warren, and they aren't married,' interjected Tony with all the superior wisdom of an eight-year-old. 'You don't have to be.'

'Oh.' Stephen looked momentarily dashed. 'It would be nice if you did, though, Dad—then Vicki would stay here for ever, wouldn't she?'

'Would you like that?' Garth asked, his grey eyes very serious as he ignored Vicki's ineffectual efforts to free herself.

'Sure I would!'

'We'll have to see about it, Stephen. I think it would be nice, too, though.' His eyes glinted wickedly as he smiled down at the red-cheeked girl in his arms. 'All we have to do is convince Vicki.'

She glared at him. 'Good luck to you,' she hissed through her teeth. 'You're the most impossible man I've ever met, do you know that?'

'She might take a bit of persuading, Stephen,' Garth drawled. 'But I'm sure we'll manage it in the end. Now—Tony and Andrew had better head home or they'll be late for supper. And I'd better carve the roast. Are you going to make gravy, Vicki?'

From a proposal of marriage to a request for gravy . . . the whole scene was rapidly turning into a farce, she thought wildly, knowing any further protests would be a waste of breath. She reached for the flour and found a wooden spoon. But then Stephen went down to the back door to see his friends off and she seized her chance, muttering fiercely, 'Do you realise what you've done? Now Stephen thinks we're going to get married—that was a dreadful thing to do!'

Garth tested the edge of the knife on his thumb. 'I never promised to fight fair, Vicki. Stephen, shut the door behind you, please, and then put water in the glasses.'

He knew perfectly well she wouldn't stage any kind of

a scene with Stephen present, Vicki thought crossly. It was too late, anyway, the damage was done.

After that conversation, to Vicki's secret consternation the evening became like any other—Stephen's homework, the usual bedtime ritual, and Garth's habitual disappearance into the study. Oppressed by a strange sense of anti-climax, she went to her room earlier than usual and read until she was tired enough to sleep.

The following Monday was Vicki's birthday. As usual, the first thing she did when she got up was to pad over to the window and look out over the ocean. It was going to be a beautiful day, for the sky was a pale cloudless blue and the sun was glittering on the water. She was twenty-one today. An adult, she thought, knowing full well that she had achieved adulthood over two years ago when it had been thrust upon her with all the pain of total disillu-sion. Today was merely a formality. Perhaps it was just as well that no one knew about it. . . .

She was just beginning preparation for supper that evening when Garth came into the kitchen. 'Leave that,' he said abruptly. 'Let's go out for a while—it's too nice a day to be indoors.'

She glanced at the clock. 'But Stephen will be home soon.'

'He's playing over at the Hunters' after school today.'

She wanted to go with him, there was no question of that. 'Just wait a second while I get my sweater.' In a couple of minutes she came back to the kitchen, wearing a heavy Arctic sweater patterned in muted shades of brown over her dark brown cords, the sweater's bulkiness em-phasising the slimness of her legs and the fragility of her wrists and hands.

They set out together, climbing up the grassy slope away from the house; a song sparrow was chirping in the woods while far below a group of gulls screamed and quarrelled over some debris the tide had left on the beach. Garth found a narrow pathway that led through the tangled undergrowth of bog laurels, Labrador tea and blueberry shrubs; he was setting a hard pace and Vicki was soon panting to keep up to him. They climbed steadily for an hour, winding their way across the hillside until they reached its peak, an untidy heap of smooth grey boulders exposed to the four winds. Only then did Garth stop, seating himself on the ground and gazing downwards. 'I love this view,' he said quietly, speaking more to himself than to her.

Vicki sat down beside him, trying to catch her breath as she looked around her. It was as though they were seated on the very summit of the world, for above was only the vast pale arc of the sky. Behind them the ancient hills and eroded, tree-clad valleys of the interior stretched as far as she could see, while in front lay the steep hillside they had traversed, the high, gaunt cliffs, and the shimmering expanse of the sea. It was almost windless, and the rays of the sun fell on her hair and skin so that she raised her face to them and shut her eyes, content to bask in the heat and to listen to the silence . . . after a while she glanced over at Garth, wanting to share her contentment with him.

He had stretched out in the grassy hollow between two rocks, pillowing his head on his jacket. His eyes were shut, and from his deep, regular breathing she knew he was asleep. Resting her cheek on her knees, she studied him thoughtfully. The long, loose-knit body. The slow rise and fall of his chest. The strength inherent in the harshly carved features that nevertheless looked oddly vulnerable in sleep. A few weeks ago she had not known he existed, yet he had altered her life in such a way that she could never go back to the Vicki she had been.

Perhaps it was the far-flung grandeur of her surroundings, or perhaps the sight of a solitary eagle soaring wild and free in the sky above that caused her to look within herself. It was not really a new discovery that she made, but rather an acknowledgment of a truth already present: she was bound to this man by ties that were fast becoming inextricable.

First there was Stephen who, she sensed, already loved

her just as she loved him. Then there was this place, whose immense, untamed beauty awoke an answering chord in herself. Finally there was Garth, in whose eyes she was beautiful. Garth, who saw through her defences to the woman who was struggling to emerge—and who wanted that woman. Again her eyes travelled the length of his body, coming to rest on the sleeping face. She could not leave him any more than she could leave Stephen, she thought dazedly, and for much the same reason. For she loved him . . . loved him with a deep and mature emotion that in some inexplicable way had become as integral a part of her as her heartbeat and as the blood that coursed through her veins.

She sat quietly, lost in the wonder of this discovery. She loved Garth. She never wanted to leave him. She would be content to spend the rest of her days at his side. And this thought gave rise to something more immediate—a longing to be physically at his side now, to lie near him and savour her new knowledge—and why not? He was still sleeping . . . with exquisite care she inched down the slope towards him and eased herself down on the grass. His even breathing continued undisturbed; his lashes lay dark and thick on his cheeks. Lying on her side so that she faced him, she raised one hand and rested it gently on his hip, where, through his jeans, she could feel the hardness of bone and sinew. She had never voluntarily touched him before. Of their own accord, her fingers slid under his sweater and felt the smoothness and warmth of his skin and then the roughness of hair. She closed her eyes and for the first time in her life she knew she had come home—everything up until now had been leading to this one perfect moment. . . .

When she opened her eyes she was looking full into Garth's, his irises a smoky, sensuous grey. Her hand was still loosely curled under his sweater, but before she could make a move his arm fell heavily across her body, trapping her, and he nuzzled his face into the curve of her throat and the softness of her hair. His kiss, when it came, had a lazy sensuality that lulled her first to submission but then to a more frank enjoyment of his closeness, of his mouth's gentle exploration of her own, of his fingers threading through the heavy fall of her hair. The sun beat down on them and far below the cold ocean waves lapped at the rocky shore.

It was Garth who spoke first. 'We'll have to continue this later,' he murmured against her ear, 'much as I hate to stop. Stephen will be getting home soon.'

Vicki had forgotten all about him. 'Oh, Garth—and I haven't got a thing ready for supper!'

'Relax—we'll find something.' He got to his feet, and reached down to help her up. Hand in hand, Vicki still in a trance of happiness, they began the downward journey. Soon the house came into sight again and Vicki exclaimed, 'Oh, look, Philip's car is there—he must have brought Stephen home. Let's hurry.' Philip was Carole's husband, whom Vicki had already met. He was a tall, thin, bearded man, several years older than his vivacious wife, with a quiet sense of humour and an easygoing manner in everything except his work, in which he was a rabid perfectionist. He was a potter, producing with his wheels and kilns a line of stoneware vases and bowls, all exquisitely shaped and glazed.

They began to run, faster and faster because of the slope of the hill, and when they finally arrived at the back door, they were both breathless and laughing. Garth pushed her into the kitchen ahead of him and to her consternation the room suddenly seemed full of people who were all singing 'Happy Birthday', and on the table was a cake with a circlet of burning candles. Vicki sagged against Garth as all the candles blurred into one flame. 'How—how did you know?' she whispered.

Carole said triumphantly, 'You told me! Don't you remember, when we were talking about horoscopes?'

'But that was ages ago.'

'Well, I remembered, and I told Garth, and we planned this together. Dinner's in the oven and as the guest of honour you're not to do a thing—we're going to wait on you for a change!'

Hovering on the brink between tears and laughter, Vicki said uncertainly, 'No one's ever done anything like this for me before. Oh dear—I need to blow my nose.'

Garth thrust a handkerchief into her hand. 'Then you'd better blow out the candles,' he grinned, tactfully ignoring her brimming eyes, 'or else you're going to have wax all over the icing.'

She blew her nose and wiped her eyes. Then she took a deep breath and to the boys' delight blew out every one of the candles. Stephen cried, 'Now unwrap your presents—there's one there from me.'

Soon there was a heap of torn paper and bright ribbon on the table. Carole and Philip had given her an exquisitely embroidered caftan of turquoise silk; Tony and Andrew a box of chocolates. From Stephen there was a wooden spice rack which he had obviously made himself, for the little shelves were not quite straight and some of the edges were rough; however, recognising it for the labour of love it undoubtedly was, she thanked him warmly. She had left Garth's present until the last; it was a small flat package that when she removed the paper turned out to be a leather jeweller's box. Her hands not quite steady, she opened the lid. On the white satin interior lay a slender gold chain with a single diamond droplet hanging from it; the light flashed and sparkled from its many facets. 'Oh, Garth,' she breathed, 'it's beautiful!'

As though they were the only two people in the room, he said seriously, 'It reminded me of the way your eyes shine when you're happy. Here, let me put it on for you.' She tipped her head forward, feeling his hands lift the thick hair from the nape of her neck. It seemed to take him a very long time. 'There,' he said finally. 'There's a little safety clasp, so it can't come undone accidentally.'

Vicki looked up to find Carole and Philip watching them both, faint, knowing smiles on their faces. She blushed and said shyly, 'It's lovely, Garth—thank you.' On impulse she reached up and kissed him full on the mouth; in his eyes as she quickly moved away she saw the

sudden flare of light, and had she but known it her own
eyes were sparkling like the jewel on her breast. 'How
long before supper, Carole?' she asked, still slightly
breathless.

'Oh, half an hour, I'd say.'

'If this is to be a party, I'm going to change,' Vicki
announced. 'That's such a pretty dress you have on,
Carole—I don't want to be wearing my cords!' She hurriedly made her escape and as she went past the dining
room she saw that the table was set with the best china
and crystal, and again her throat almost closed with
emotion, for she knew most of it must be Carole's doing—
Carole who was over eight months pregnant and had a
family of her own, yet could still find time and energy to
arrange a surprise party for a new friend.

It did not take her long to decide what to wear. It was
a dress she had made herself of soft white wool, a classic
shirtwaister with a full skirt narrowing to a belted waist,
and long sleeves gathered to tight cuffs; the diamond
droplet looked perfect in the deep 'V' of the neckline. She
brushed her hair into a loose chignon at her nape, put on
her high-heeled shoes and dabbed perfume at her throat
and wrists. About to leave the room, she hesitated briefly,
looking gravely at her own reflection in the long mirror
by the door, her fingers toying with the slim gold chain.
She had the feeling as far as Garth was concerned that
events were rushing to a climax and for one dreadful
moment all the old fears returned, mocking her new pride
of bearing and her fragile beauty—what if Garth were no
different from Barry? What then?

'Vicki? Your sherry's poured.'

Garth's voice. Calling her. It seemed somehow symbolic, and recklessly she smiled at herself in the mirror
before stepping out into the hall.

CHAPTER EIGHT

GARTH was waiting for her, a thin-stemmed crystal glass in one hand. 'Oh, there you——' he broke off, his eyes taking in every detail of her appearance. 'You must wear that dress when we marry, Vicki—I've never seen you look lovelier.'

Again she had that sensation of being swept along towards some unknown destination. 'Garth, we can't——'

He silenced her half-hearted protest with a kiss. 'Dinner's nearly ready,' he said calmly. 'We'll talk later.'

The meal was delicious: piping hot lasagne, a tossed salad and garlic bread served with a full-bodied red wine, then birthday cake and ice cream. Afterwards the three boys settled on the floor with a game and the adults sat around the fire drinking coffee and liqueurs, talking with all the ease of old friends. Philip had been telling them that he had been invited to send some pieces to a prestigious exhibition to be held in Toronto, and Vicki asked curiously, 'Have you always been interested in pottery, Philip? Since you were a boy, I mean?'

'No—not at all. My father was determined I should become a partner in the family law firm, so I was packed off to law school—I knew it wasn't right, but I didn't know what I wanted in its place. Then I met Carole, we fell in love and married. By one of those peculiar chances that can have such a profound effect on one's life, our car broke down on our honeymoon and when we went to the only house in sight—this was in New Hampshire, miles from anywhere—the owner turned out to be a potter, one of the best known in the eastern States. After that, I knew exactly what I wanted, although it wasn't always easy because I had so much to learn.'

'But you were so much happier, Phil, in clay up to your wrists, than you'd ever been trying to study those dry old law books,' Carole put in. 'Luckily I'd been left some money by my grandmother, so at least we didn't starve!'

Philip smiled at her lovingly. 'I always told you I married you for your money, darling.'

'So you did,' Carole laughed. 'What a dreadful thing to do to a woman, don't you agree, Vicki?'

The colour drained from Vicki's face and her fingers clenched so tightly around her glass that the stem snapped. She gave a tiny, shocked exclamation as the clear syrupy liquid trickled over her hand and mingled with the blood from her cut palm. In an instant Garth was at her side, carefully removing the other pieces of glass and putting them on the hearth. Holding her hand in both of his, he ordered, 'Come to the bathroom—I'll have to wash the cut out to make sure there's no glass in it.'

Carole asked anxiously, 'Can I help? How on earth did it happen, Vic?'

'I—I don't know. Maybe it was cracked,' Vicki faltered, hoping her undoubted pallor would be put down to the shock of her injury rather than to anything that had been said. But as Garth gently held her palm over the sink to examine it, she soon realised that he, at least, had not been deceived.

'You had money, did you?' he said conversationally. 'And that's why Barry married you?'

Wondering if she was going to be sick, for she felt deathly cold, she managed to say, 'I don't want to talk about it.'

'Once we're alone later this evening, that's just what we're going to talk about,' he said relentlessly. 'You've been hiding things for too long.' He unscrewed the bottle of disinfectant. 'Hold on—this will hurt.'

Vicki drew in her breath as the disinfectant penetrated the cut, watching numbly as Garth taped on a neat covering of gauze. 'That feels better,' she said, carefully flexing her palm.

'Are you all right?'

She nodded, knowing he was not only referring to her

hand. 'Yes—let's go back. I don't want Carole to worry.'

It was nearly ten by the time the Hunters had gone home and Stephen was asleep. With some misgivings Vicki saw Garth put another log on the fire. 'Garth, I'm tired,' she said. 'I think I'll go to bed.'

He straightened. 'No, Vicki—this has waited long enough. It's not going to be put off again.'

'You're making a fuss about nothing,' she retorted.

'You didn't break that glass for nothing. You broke it because Phil made a remark about marrying a woman for her money. And now you're going to tell me how that applies to you.'

In an angry swirl of white skirts she perched herself on the arm of the chair nearest the fire. 'All right!' she blazed. 'I was in love with Barry. But I found out after we were married that the only reason he married me was because I'd inherited a sizeable amount of money. So I'd made a fool of myself—and unfortunately everyone in the office knew about it.' She stood up and the flickering flames in the hearth were caught in the diamond at her throat. 'So now you know—and now I'm going to bed.'

But as she stalked past him his arm lashed out and caught her round the waist, swinging her round to face him. 'No, Vicki—because you haven't even begun.'

'There's nothing more to tell.'

'How much money? And who left it to you?'

'A great-aunt who'd been living in British Columbia. I didn't even know she'd existed. It was over a hundred thousand dollars.'

His eyes widened. 'That much? What did Barry need it for?'

Her anger evaporated and her body sagged in his hold as she stared down at the fire, her brown eyes bitter. 'Business,' she said succinctly. 'He'd pulled a few shady deals and he needed some quick money if he wasn't going to get caught. So he used mine.'

'How did you meet?'

Scarcely noticing what was happening, she allowed herself to be guided back to her seat; Garth sat facing her

on the hearth, watching her closely. 'When I moved to
Montreal I didn't have much money. There seemed to be
quite a demand for secretaries, so I took a typing course
and got a job in the typing pool of a big shipping firm
where Barry was one of the junior executives.' More than
half the girls had been crazy about him, she remembered.
He had been good-looking, well-dressed, charming and
witty. She herself was hopelessly in love with him before a
month was out, focussing on him all her adolescent dreams
and longings; he, of course, had not even noticed her existence. Then had come the letter from her great-aunt's
solicitors with the news of her good fortune. She had told
one of her friends in the typing pool and suddenly everyone knew. A week later, when she had stayed behind to
finish a couple of invoices, Barry had asked her out for
dinner. At the time she had thought it a coincidence that
he too should have been working late.

'He asked me to have dinner with him. It was only six
weeks from the time of our first date until we got
married—I, of course, was tremendously flattered, thinking he couldn't wait to marry me.' She laughed cynically.
'It was my money he couldn't wait for. We'd put it all in
a joint account—after all, why not? I loved him ... he
was going to be my husband. Within two weeks half of it
was gone. At first, because I was stupid enough to trust
him, I believed all his fine talk about investments and
trust funds and what have you. But then we went to a
party at one of his friends'. . . .'

Their marriage had been a succession of parties, she
recalled, always with the same crowd, always involving
too much of everything: food, drink, noise, reckless driving. How she had come to hate them by the time Barry
died! She and he had rarely ever gone anywhere alone
together; she could not conceive, for instance, of Barry
walking with her up a lonely hillside and then peacefully
falling asleep in the sun.

'To make a long story short,' she said wearily, 'Barry
drank too much that evening and before we went home I
overheard him telling a friend how clever he'd been to

get his hands on all that money—although it was a pity he'd had to marry me to do so, because I was such a boring little provincial, so square and old-fashioned and dull. The friend worked for the same firm, so of course in no time the word got around. Barry hadn't wanted me to quit my job, so I was still working there, you see.' Her voice raw with remembered pain, she said, 'It was so humiliating—I hated it! I wanted to leave, but I was making a reasonable salary by then and Barry was going through the money so fast I was afraid to quit.'

'Was he faithful to you?'

She flinched. 'What do *you* think? No, of course he wasn't. I found out about that at the same party I was telling you about. He had one girl-friend in particular—everyone knew about her, too.'

'One more question, Vicki—how did he die?'

'Coming home from one of the clubs in the middle of the night after he'd had too much to drink. He skidded taking a corner and drove straight into a cement wall at seventy miles an hour.' She shuddered. 'Driving the car that he'd bought with my money.'

'Poetic justice.'

There was such repressed savagery in his tone that Vicki looked full at him. 'Are you angry with me?' she faltered.

'God, no—not with you. Maybe it's just as well he's not around. I'd like to horsewhip him!' He ran his fingers through his hair. 'More questions,' he rapped. 'How old were you when you met him?'

'Eighteen.' She grimaced. 'A very young eighteen at that.'

'Did he leave you any money?'

'By the time I'd sorted everything out and paid all the debts—because, among other things, he'd neglected to pay the car insurance—I had exactly four thousand dollars left. I had to get out of that office and out of Montreal, Garth. So I decided to take a year and try my hand at writing, living as cheaply as I could.'

'Would you have divorced him?'

She hesitated for a long moment, staring down at her

slender, ringless fingers. 'I don't think so,' she said in a low voice. 'You see, I loved him when I married him, and the promises I made were promises for life.' Inconsequently she added, 'One of the worst things about it all was the feeling of relief after he was dead. It was as though I'd awoken from a dreadful nightmare. I was sorry he died, because he was young and it seemed such a waste—but I couldn't be sorry that he was out of my life.'

'So you felt guilty instead.'

'Yes,' she said, knowing he understood.

'So what you've told me is the basis for your reluctance to marry again—or to get seriously involved with another man. . . .'

'Well, of course,' she agreed impatiently. 'It's simple—I was taken in. I made a complete fool of myself. I thought the sun rose and set on Barry—and all the time he was using me and laughing at me behind my back.'

Garth leaned forward, his eyes intent. The firelight flickered over his face. 'You had a very bad experience, Vicki—and a particularly difficult one to assimilate as you were so young and had nothing else to compare it with. But you can't let it ruin your whole life. Trite as it may sound, not all men are like Barry.'

'I daresay. But how do I *know*? Don't you see? My judgment was completely off as far as he was concerned. So now I can't even trust that.'

'You certainly won't learn to trust it by shutting off all your emotions and living like a nun,' he countered sharply.

If only he knew! That it was he who had forced her to life again—that it was he whom she loved.

He must have taken her silence for disagreement. 'So you made a mistake, Vicki,' he persisted. 'That's a perfectly normal part of being human.' There was a sudden bitter twist to his mouth. 'Do you think I never made one? We're none of us immune to that.'

He got up, stretching to his full height, and began restlessly pacing up and down the carpet, his hands thrust in his pockets, and intuitively she sensed that his own demons were pursuing him. So when he spoke his words came as a complete surprise. He came to a halt in front of her, his face stern, his grey eyes hard with purpose. 'This has gone on long enough.'

She blinked. 'What has?' she said blankly.

'You know damn well why I brought you here—I was perfectly open about it.'

Her heart began to bang against her ribs. 'I came as Stephen's housekeeper,' she answered with assumed coolness.

'We're talking about you and me right now—not about Stephen.'

Poised in front of her, he looked as dangerous and as unpredictable as a mountain cat about to strike. She waited, her throat dry. The fear that had attacked her in the bedroom was back again in full force and as though she was his prey she began to tremble, her wide-held eyes very dark.

'I brought you here to marry you. Tomorrow I'll go to Sydney and get a special licence—there's only a three-day waiting period.'

She remained silent, trying desperately to still her shaking limbs.

'What if I say no?' she asked finally, amazed at how steady her voice sounded.

His fists clenched at his sides. 'Don't,' he said threateningly. 'You have no reason to say no—believe me, I'm not like Barry.'

'No,' she said slowly, 'you're as different from Barry as anyone could be.' For Garth was a man of depth and subtlety, whereas Barry had been all on the surface, his charm that of a spoiled child. 'I don't need to marry you to know that.'

'You need to marry me to learn trust again. And joy and laughter and sharing.'

But not love, she thought numbly, knowing that of all omissions that was the unforgivable one. He was not saying he loved her, nor was he promising to love her in the future. So how could she agree to marry him?

'I know I can make you happy again, Vicki. But you've got to trust me.'

Following her own train of thought she said, 'The days are long gone when you could drag me to the altar against my will.'

The eyes narrowed and in spite of herself she shivered. 'That's true,' he said silkily. 'But there are other ways of doing it. You say you came here as the housekeeper—housekeepers can be fired, you know. You'd have to leave. Maybe you wouldn't find it difficult to leave me—but could you leave Stephen?'

Ashen-pale, she whispered, 'You wouldn't be so cruel.'

'I want you, Vicki. And I mean to have you. I've tried to be reasonable and I've certainly tried to understand how badly hurt you were by Barry. But my patience won't last for ever.'

'Even knowing I was violently opposed to it, you'd still marry me?'

'Yes—because I know I can change you.'

She closed her eyes. Her palm was throbbing and she felt very tired. 'So there are two alternatives,' she said emotionlessly. 'I can marry you in three days—or I can leave.'

'Yes.'

Slowly she pushed herself upright. 'I shall give you my answer tomorrow morning,' she said. 'I promise you that much. In the meantime I'm going to bed. Goodnight, Garth.'

For a heart-stopping moment she thought he was going to prevent her from leaving. His eyes were likes stones, his mouth a thin line, and she felt anger emanating from him like a visible force; if there was pain underlying the anger, she was too confused to see it. But then he deliberately stepped back. 'Goodnight, Vicki,' he said, each word touching her skin like a flick of a whip.

Her room was a sanctuary of privacy and peace, the distant murmur of the ocean as soothing as a hand strok-ing her brow. From behind the house the moon was throwing a silver light over the sea; the headlands, in contrast, were the impenetrable black of ink. She sank down on the thick carpet, hugging her knees and deliberately emptying her mind, and after a while she grew calmer. Moving very quietly, she showered and put on her new caftan, its barbaric colours and sweep of fabric further raising her morale. Once again she went to sit by the window.

Two choices: leave here or marry Garth. So simple and so abominably difficult. For it was not just a question of leaving Stephen, although that would be an intolerable wrench; she would also be leaving Garth, with his paradoxical blend of gentleness and ruthlessness, perception and blindness. She had been so sure of her happiness up on the hillside when she had realised she loved him; that certainty was gone now and her joy was tainted by fear.

Six weeks she had known Barry before she had married him. She had been deliriously happy, caught up in the magic of a dream come true. And the dream, as she had told Garth, had all too soon become a nightmare.

She had known Garth for much the same length of time. Now, when she looked back, she knew she had been attracted to him from the beginning, but that she had fought against this attraction every inch of the way. Tonight she had still been fighting. Although he was in most ways very different from Barry, in one respect they were alike: Garth was not telling the whole truth about why he wanted to marry her. Something was hidden. Some motive unknown to her was driving him to claim her. . . .

The house was very quiet. As silently as a ghost she opened her door and tiptoed across the dimly lit hallway to Stephen's room. He was lying flat on his back, arms outspread, a stuffed animal against his cheek. He looked so like his father that her breath caught in her throat and suddenly the decision was made. She was lost—she could not possibly leave. She would marry Garth, trusting her newly discovered love to guide her in a relationship whose complexities, she already sensed, would be far more subtle, far more dangerous, than any of those with Barry.

A strange kind of peace fell over her and her hands

were very gentle as she pulled up the blankets and covered
the sleeping boy. She bent and kissed him on the cheek,
resting her fingers on his tousled hair.

Not until she turned to leave the room did she see
Garth. He was standing in the door, wearing a belted
robe that left his legs and feet bare; she had no idea how
long he had been there. As she glided towards him, he
moved back to let her pass. A tiny night-light cast a dim
glow over his features; his eyes were shadowed and bleak,
and with a new sensitivity Vicki divined the almost unbearable tension that he was disguising behind a harsh,
uncaring mask. 'You haven't slept,' she said softly.

'Nor have you.'

She smiled faintly. 'No.' She hesitated. 'Do you know
what I'd like—a cup of tea.'

Because she loved him, she was relieved to see the sombre
lines of his face dissolve into a smile. 'That's easy
enough—let's go to the kitchen and make one.'

She put on the kettle and Garth took out a couple of
mugs, pouring the milk and adding a little sugar to hers;
he looked very tired. Because he had given her until tomorrow morning for her answer, she knew he would not
mention the subject of their marriage tonight. Equally
she knew she wanted to erase the strain from his features.
'Garth?' she said tentatively.

He glanced up. She found herself wondering if he was
wearing anything under the brief robe—she rather
doubted that he was. She swallowed hard. 'Garth, if you
still want me, I'll marry you.'

He made an instinctive move towards her and then
checked himself. 'You don't have to tell me now—you've
got until tomorrow.'

'I know—but I won't change my mind.'

'That was why you went to see Stephen ... to help
make your decision.' There was a bite to his voice.

'Partly. . . .' It was not working; the harsh lines were
still engraved from cheek to chin. 'Aren't you pleased?'

He started to say something, then stopped. There was a
noticeable pause. 'Of course I am. It's just—oh hell,

Vicki, of course I'm pleased. And Stephen will be delighted—but I'm sure you've already thought of that.'

She had a sinking feeling in the pit of her stomach. She was not sure how she'd expected Garth to behave now that she had finally capitulated—but his almost offhand manner was the last thing she would have anticipated. She gave a nervous laugh. 'Maybe you've changed your mind—you don't seem very enthusiastic.'

'No,' he said shortly, 'I haven't changed my mind.'

The kettle was boiling and she was glad to have something to do. She made the tea and set the Pyrex teapot on the stove. 'Do you want anything to eat?' she asked, wanting to break his stony-faced silence.

'No, thanks.'

She was crazy, she thought miserably. She must be, for she had just agreed to marry a man with whom she couldn't even communicate. . . . 'I know so little about you, Garth,' she blurted.

'You know all the important things. We have a lifetime ahead of us to fill in the rest.'

'I've told you quite a bit about Barry, but you haven't said anything about your wife.'

'Corinne?' He gave a short, ugly laugh. 'I don't want to talk about her, Vicki—especially not to you. She's dead and gone and buried, and the marriage with her.'

'But you loved her.' It was more of a statement than a question.

'Oh yes, I loved her.'

And you don't love me, she continued silently. Lucky Corinne, to be loved by you. Lucky, lucky Corinne. . . .

As if he had read her mind, Garth said quietly, 'It'll be all right, Vicki—our marriage, I mean. You'll see.'

'I hope so. I—I want it to be.' It was as close as she dared come to saying she wanted to make him happy.

He got up, resting his hands on her shoulders. 'Would you mind very much if we didn't go away for a honeymoon right away? For Stephen's sake it might be just as well to stay around here. Normally I'd have suggested leaving him at the Hunters', but Carole's baby is nearly due and it seems a bit much to ask.'

'I love it here—I don't mind not going away.' A honeymoon was the last thing she wanted.

'But we'll ask Carole and Philip to stand with us, shall we? Or do you want a big wedding?'

'No!' she said so vehemently that he laughed.

'We're agreed on that, then. You'll wear the dress you had on this evening?'

To be discussing the practical aspects of their wedding seemed to bring it alarmingly near. Vicki fingered the slender gold chain around her neck to give herself courage. 'If you like.'

'The whole thing doesn't sound very romantic, I'm afraid,' Garth said doubtfully. 'All you'll be doing is moving your things from your room to mine.'

She tensed. 'We'll share a room, will we?'

He raised his eyebrows. 'I should hope so,' he said drily. 'Don't you remember my list of reasons?'

She remembered it only too well. Avoiding his eyes, she felt the old familiar panic race along her nerves. 'I want you,' he had said—and in three days he would be legally entitled to take her, whether she was willing or not. His hands were still on her shoulders and their weight seemed to be crushing her.

'I wish we were married now,' he said huskily. 'If we were, I'd take you to my room.' His hands slid down her back and she saw his eyes ignite as he discovered that under the long silken robe she was naked. 'I would undress you and then we'd make love.' He undid the clasp at the neckline of her caftan and slowly slid the zipper down to her waist. She stood mute and unprotesting; every muscle in her body seemed to be frozen. With a deliberation that terrified her in its very restraint, he pushed the edges of the robe apart and his palms cupped her breasts, stroking the softness of her flesh until she thought she would faint. He kissed each rosy tip, and without her volition, each nipple pulsed and hardened to his touch. A shudder rippled along her nerves. Then, just as deliberately, he covered her again and his lips found her mouth. When he released her, she was trembling.

'Beautiful Vicki,' he murmured. 'I don't want to start anything I can't stop.' His eyes smouldered. 'We only have to wait three days—at the moment it seems forever, but it'll be over before we know it. And now you'd better go to bed. Get lots of sleep the next few nights, won't you? Because once I have you in my bed, you won't get much.'

Hidden by the folds of her robe, her hands clenched to fists as she fought to subdue the shivering of her flesh. Three days, she thought, appalled. Only three days, and the worst secret from her past, the one bitter humiliation that she had shared with no one, would confront her— would confront them both. It could not be avoided; equally she could not bear to contemplate it. She was trapped . . . because of that small word love she was once again trapped.

'Don't look at me like that!' he said sharply.

She made an attempt to smile, knowing she would do anything to delay the inevitable moment of truth. 'Sorry. . . .' Her laugh sounded almost credible. 'Pre-nuptial nerves, Garth. I'll be all right.'

'You're sure it's no more than that?' His eyes scanned her face mercilessly and she forced herself to meet them without flinching.

'Of course not—what else could it be?' she said lightly.

'Perhaps I wasn't expecting you to be nervous, as this is the second time round for you. It's not as though you're totally inexperienced.'

There was a sharpness in his voice that disconcerted her, making it impossible for her to say what was on the tip of her tongue: that complete inexperience could well be preferable to an accumulation of bad experiences. But he was still talking. . . .

'No last-minute thoughts about changing your mind?'

Staring straight ahead of her she said steadily, 'I won't change my mind—I made a promise to you and Stephen, and I'll keep that promise.'

'Come hell or high water, eh?'

Frightened by the savagery of his tone, she said with

attempted lightness, 'A promise is a promise.'

'And what if it were just me?'

'What do you mean?'

'What if Stephen didn't exist—would you still keep your promise—or would you have made it in the first place?'

Dangerous ground. 'That's purely theoretical, Garth, so how can I answer it? Stephen does exist,' she said with assumed calmness. 'He's your son, a part of you—how can I separate the two of you?'

He banged his palm against the edge of the table. 'Whether you know it or not, you are answering,' he said grimly. 'I'm getting the message—no Stephen, no marriage. I'm right, aren't I?'

'What difference does it make?' she burst out.

'If you don't know, far be it from me to tell you.'

She scarcely heard him. 'You know as well as I do that Stephen needs a woman's care and love—surely you don't begrudge him that?'

'No, of course I don't,' he snapped. 'This is a useless conversation, Vicki, let's end it. You'd better go to bed.'

Her nerves jangling, she moved towards the door. 'Goodnight, Garth,' she said faintly.

He was staring out of the window into the darkness, his shoulders a taut line. 'Goodnight,' he said brusquely, and she knew she had been dismissed.

Garth was gone most of the next day, returning just before supper to tell Vicki that all the formalities had been completed and they would be married on Friday evening. He had hardly finished speaking when Stephen came running into the kitchen. 'Hi, Dad! Where were you?'

Garth answered with a question of his own. 'Is it all right with you if Vicki and I get married on Friday?'

'Really?' asked Stephen, wide-eyed.

'Really.'

Stephen looked over at the silently watching girl. 'You'd always be here then, wouldn't you? You'd be like a real mother?'

'Yes, Stephen.' It was as though she was promising him something.

The little boy grinned. 'That'd be great. Why do you have to wait until Friday?'

'My reasoning exactly,' Garth drawled, noticing Vicki's heightened colour with sardonic amusement. 'Unfortunately it's the law, Stephen. Listen, let's eat supper and go over to the Hunters'—we should check whether they'll be free Friday evening.'

With a strange sense of fatalism Vicki saw the net drawing ever tighter. First Garth, then Stephen, and now the Hunters. . . .

'By the way,' Garth put in, 'do you want to invite Nils?'

Disconcerted, she stared at him. 'I haven't heard from him since I came up here,' she said uncertainly. Nils would be less than pleased to hear of her impending marriage, she thought, and rightly so, for not that long ago she had assured him she would never marry again. . . . 'I guess not,' she murmured finally. 'But I'll drop him a letter in the mail telling him about it. It's funny he hasn't come for a visit.'

'Okay—I just thought I'd check. Stephen, wash your hands before supper.'

A couple of hours later they were all three standing on the Hunters' doorstep as Stephen rapped the brass knocker. Philip opened the door. 'Hello—what a nice surprise,' he said cordially. 'Come in. The boys are in the playroom, Stephen. And Carole's in the living room with her feet up—she'll be pleased to see you.'

Six years ago Philip and Carole had bought an old farmhouse and in the intervening period had almost completely remodelled it. However, they had purposely kept the old-fashioned atmosphere by preserving the beamed ceilings, the small square windowpanes, and the worn softwood floors, and their furniture was in keeping: pine antiques and colourful handwoven rugs and draperies. A pot of rust-coloured beech leaves and native grasses stood in one corner, while the firelight cast a friendly glow over everything.

'Don't get up, Carole,' said Garth. 'How are you feeling?'

With a comical grimace Carole looked down at herself. 'Huge! But otherwise fine. Come and sit down, Vicki—what have you been up to all day?'

Before Vicki could answer, Garth said smoothly, 'As a matter of fact, she's been gettting herself engaged.'

'What?' Carole shrieked.

Garth grinned. 'You heard—Vicki and I are going to be married.'

'Well,' said Carole with more truth than tact, 'you're a fast worker, Garth Travis. What did he do, Vicki, sweep you off your feet?'

'More or less,' she responded weakly, knowing it was the literal truth but unable to say so.

'When's the big day?' Philip intervened.

'Friday evening,' Garth replied. 'In fact, that's why we're here—we'd like you both to come. Will you be my best man, Phil?'

'I'd be delighted to.' A smile of genuine warmth lit up his lean, ascetic face. 'Delighted . . . I guess I don't need to tell you you're a lucky man, Garth?'

'No,' Garth said very quietly, 'you don't need to tell me that, Phil.'

Vicki blushed, looking touchingly young in her flared skirt and angora sweater; on her breast the diamond twinkled and shone as she met Garth's eyes squarely. 'I'm lucky, too,' she said, feeling quite inexplicably as though she wanted to cry. As if they were alone in the room, Garth favoured her with that rare smile that softened his granite-grey eyes.

'Oh dear,' Carole wailed, 'I feel all sentimental and dewy-eyed! Pass me a handkerchief, Phil.'

The emotion was released in laughter, and Philip went over to the tall wooden cabinet that stood on one corner. 'This calls for a drink—we should have champagne, but I think you'll have to settle for sherry or a liqueur.'

As Garth went to help him, Carole said softly to Vicki, 'I hope you'll be very happy, dear. You're far too young to be widowed and on your own—now you'll have a ready-made family with Stephen, and I'm sure you and Garth will have children of your own.' Her eyes lingered on her tall, bearded husband, standing by the cabinet talking to Garth. 'There's nothing more fulfilling in this world than living with the man you love and then bearing his child.'

Even if he doesn't love you? Vicki wondered, Carole's words piercing her with a bittersweet pain; for if Carole loved Philip, equally Philip loved Carole. What if all the love was one-sided—what then?

Perhaps fortunately, she had no chance to phrase her question openly, for Philip was putting a glass in her hand and the conversation became general. 'What time on Friday?' Carole asked.

'Seven—at St John's Church at the Bay.'

'You'll come here afterwards for a while,' Carole announced. 'And Stephen can stay here overnight.'

Garth laughed. 'That's very understanding of you, Carole—thanks!'

Vicki should have been equally pleased by this offer, but somehow she was not—perhaps subconsciously she had been counting on Stephen's presence in the house Friday night as some kind of protection. She took a sip of sherry, avoiding Garth's eyes, but if he noticed that she did not add her thanks to his, his said nothing. Before long they were on their way home, in order that the boys could get to bed at the normal time. Once Stephen was settled, Garth said matter-of-factly, 'I'm going to have to work the next couple of evenings, Vicki. I've got a deadline on this book and I'm running behind. Sorry about that.'

'That's all right—I understand.' Secretly she was relieved, for with the knowledge of what lay ahead it was becoming less and less possible to relax in his presence.

CHAPTER NINE

SLOWLY the days passed. Tuesday, Wednesday, Thursday, and tomorrow would be Vicki's wedding day. Garth had left the study only for meals on Thursday, and by ten o'clock in the evening she finally decided she might as well go to bed.

In her room she slipped on her nightgown and robe, then put out the light and went to sit in her favourite place by the window where she could see the vast sweep of the ocean and the blacker pit of the sky. But tonight they failed to work their usual magic. The waves, rather than soothing her, seemed to be whispering warnings, telling her to run while she still could. The darkness dwarfed her, mocking her with its immensity. She felt very much alone.

Later she heard the sound of Garth's footsteps down the deserted hallway. Did they pause briefly outside her door? She huddled into the soft fabric of her robe, longing for him to come in, dreading that he might. Then the footsteps passed on and his door closed quietly. Tomorrow night when that door closed, she would be in Garth's room with him; she would no longer be able to escape to the privacy of her own bedroom. She would belong to him, body and soul. . . .

No longer able to stand her own thoughts, she got into bed, pulling the covers around her like a cocoon. Although for a long time she lay awake, staring into the darkness, eventually she must have slept, for when she next opened her eyes it was with the sensation of having been jerked back to consciousness. All she could hear was the pounding of her own heart. It was pitch dark. Straining ears and eyes, she caught a whisper of movement, a patterning of shadows on the pale carpet, and her breath caught in her throat. Sitting up, she faltered, 'Who is it?'

She heard a harsh sigh. 'Vicki? You're there?'

She straightened as Garth sat heavily on the bed. 'What's wrong? Is Stephen——?'

'Stephen's fine.'

Her eyes were more used to the dark now and she could distinguish his bowed back, his head resting on his hands. Forgetting that she was frightened of him, she rested a hand on his shoulder. 'Garth, tell me what's the matter.'

'God! This is going to sound ridiculous——' He swung round to face her. 'I was dreaming—one of those dreams where the real and the unreal are mixed and you can't separate them. We were to be married, you and I, but you didn't go the church and when I went looking for you, you'd gone. I went from room to room in the house and they were all empty, and with each empty room I became more and more certain that I would never find you. At the end I was running, but my legs felt like lead and I knew I was too late. . . .'

Compassion washed over her. So Garth was not as sure of her as he would appear—and needed her more than he would admit. She opened her arms and his own arms came hard around her as though he had to prove to himself that she was real, not a creature of dreams.

Gently Vicki rocked him back and forth, feeling the weight of his head on her breast. 'I'm here,' she murmured. 'And I'll be here tomorrow when it's time for us to get married—I promise.'

She felt his lips move against her skin as he spoke. 'I'm sorry I woke you up. But I just had to make sure the dream was over, that you hadn't gone away.'

She said lightly, 'You're not getting rid of me that easily!'

He pushed himself upright, his eyes deep-shadowed. 'Don't joke about it,' he said hoarsely. 'If you think I want to get rid of you, you're crazy. I want you so much I can hardly sleep. And when I do, I dream about you.'

She said weakly, 'I guess I was just trying to reassure you.'

She could feel him hesitate. Then he said, 'Vicki, will

you do something for me?'

This did not seem to be the time to waver or make conditions. 'Yes,' she gulped.

'Will you let me lie down beside you for a while?' He must have sensed her recoil. 'Don't be frightened. I promise I won't start anything we can't stop. I'm old-fashioned enough that I want us to make love for the first time on our wedding night. I just want to hold you and make sure you're real, then I'll go back to my own room.'

She had to trust that he meant what he said. Under those conditions, there could be no harm in it, could there? 'Well I—all right.'

She lay down again on her side facing him. His robe fell to the floor and then he was sliding under the covers, and a shock raced through her as she felt his naked length pressed against her body. She lay very still, gradually becoming aware of separate sensations—warmth, hardness, the tantalisingly masculine scent of his skin. Gradually she began to relax. He had let one arm fall across her hip and it lay there, pinioning her had she wanted to struggle. But she did not want to. True to his word, he was doing nothing but lying quietly beside her, and it gradually came to her that she could trust his word. Lulled by his steady breathing, made drowsy by the combined heat of their two bodies, she felt herself slipping off into sleep again, and her last conscious thought was that tomorrow night might not be so bad after all. . . .

Her head dropped on to his shoulder, her hair spreading over his skin like a dark, sweet-scented fan. The man held her more closely, although by a rigid control Vicki had not appreciated his hands remained slack and immobile on her body. It was very late when he eased himself free of her and silently left the room.

So when Vicki awoke the next morning, she was alone in the big bed. As her eyes opened, they flew to the pillow beside her with its tell-tale indentation, and she knew she had not dreamed that brief interlude of closeness and warmth; Garth had come to her room and shared her bed. Tonight they would share a bed again—but tonight he would not be content to merely lie beside her. She buried her face in the pillow, trying to shut out the first sounds of the household stirring to life: the hiss of the shower, Stephen's high-pitched voice calling something to his father. She was not ready, she thought, panic-stricken. Not ready to become Garth's wife and face his inevitable demands on her. Why, oh, why had she ever agreed to this hasty marriage?

A token tap of the door and Stephen burst in. 'It's today you're getting married, isn't it? I wish I didn't have to go to school!'

'We're not getting married until this evening,' Vicki said, surprised to notice how matter-of-fact her voice sounded.

'I know, but I might miss something. Dad has a surprise for you——' he clapped his hands over his mouth. 'I wasn't supposed to say anything about it!'

A disconcertingly normal beginning to the day: breakfast around the kitchen table, the usual chatter, packing Stephen's lunch, seeing him off to the bus. Garth had come to stand beside Vicki as she waved goodbye, and as the little figure in its bright blue jacket disappeared from sight, he said soberly, 'If it hadn't been for you, I wouldn't be standing here doing this, Vicki—because I wouldn't have a son.' His arm came to rest on her shoulder. 'I'll never be able to thank you enough.'

She stood absolutely still. It had never occurred to her before that his motive for marrying her might be gratitude, and gratitude alone. 'Is that why you're marrying me?'

He turned her to face him. 'Is that what you think?'

'I don't know what to think,' she said miserably.

'Because you rescued Stephen, I know about your courage and intelligence, and they are qualities I admire in you, Vicki. But to say I'm marrying you just because I'm grateful—no, that wouldn't be right.'

'I see,' she said in a small voice.

'I'm not sure you do.' He looked straight into her eyes, his own a deep, smoky grey. 'But don't worry about it, my dear. In time you'll come to understand.'

Trust ... he was asking her to trust him. So easy to ask, so difficult to do. She gazed down the hill at the ocean. There was a light breeze blowing onshore and at the base of the cliffs the waves curled crisp and white, a lace edging to the flat blue sheet of the ocean. Beneath her feet was new green grass; beside the house the crocuses were in bloom, gold and purple and white; from the hill-side came the ecstatic thrills of the song sparrows. A fine spring day, a day of promise and fresh beginnings.

His change of subject took her by surprise. Reaching down, he picked up her left hand in his much larger one. 'I haven't been able to get you an engagement ring,' he said abruptly. 'I hope in a couple of weeks we can take a weekend to go to a city and do some shopping.' He rubbed her ringless finger with the ball of his thumb, his head bent. 'Did Barry give you a ring?'

'Yes, he did,' she said evenly. 'He told me it was a family heirloom and had belonged to his grandmother. I found out later he'd bought it at a pawnshop—with my money, of course. So please don't worry about engagement rings.'

It was as though her openness encouraged him to an equal honesty. 'There'll be no family heirlooms from me. Everything I own I've worked for myself.'

He so rarely said anything that related to his personal life that she picked her words with care, not wanting to drive him back into his shell. 'You've never mentioned your family.'

'With good reason.'

'Won't you tell me about them now?'

Shutting the back door, Garth walked back into the kitchen and poured himself a second cup of coffee. Not looking at her, he began to talk, his voice clipped and emotionless. 'My mother was one of ten children born to a Montreal dockworker. She left home at fifteen and got work in a factory. My father was a stoker on one of the ocean liners that called in at Montreal. They were married when my mother was only sixteen. My father was trying to get a shore job so they could be together all the time, when he was killed in a boiler explosion; five months later I was born.'

Deeply distressed, Vicki murmured, 'So you never knew your father at all.'

'No. I have a photograph of him, that's all. My mother used to tell me about him as I was growing up—I would have liked to have known him.'

'Whatever did she do—all alone with a new baby to look after?'

'It was a bitterly hard struggle for her, because there was nowhere she could go for help—her own parents were dead by then. She was a live-in kitchenmaid at first, and then later went back to the factory once I started school. She was determined I get an education and she worked her fingers to the bone for me—by the time she was thirty, she looked forty-five.'

He fell silent, his grey eyes bleak. 'What happened?' Vicki asked gently.

'She died when I was fourteen. Pneumonia, the doctors called it. What they should have said was poverty—overwork, never enough to eat or enough warm clothes.' In a gesture of savage frustration he indicated their luxurious surroundings. 'If only she could have lived long enough to enjoy all this!'

So he had not always been a man of wealth and he would never take this luxury for granted. He could remember grinding poverty in the back streets of Montreal, and from an upbringing whose hardships she could only partly appreciate had sprung his toughness, his need for privacy—and equally his compassion and his strength. . . . 'What did you do when she died?'

'Oh, I knocked around Montreal for a while, taking on odd jobs, lying about my age so I wouldn't get shoved in an orphanage. Then I went to sea for three years, and after that I settled down and took a few university courses and started writing.'

She could imagine him all too clearly at fourteen—already tall and angular, with a crop of thick dark hair, his face knowledgeable beyond his years, his hooded eyes hiding what must have been a corrosive loneliness. He had had to be hard and resourceful to survive, and that ruthless drive was still in him. He was not a man to brook obstacles. He had wanted *her*, hadn't he? And now he was getting her.

Not knowing what else to say, she murmured, 'Stephen, at least, will have a very different upbringing. Between us, we can give him all the love and security you lacked.'

Garth rubbed his forehead with his fingers. 'Yes,' he said flatly, 'that's true enough. I know how much you care for him.'

And for you too, her heart cried out.

'Well, I'd better head for the study. I have to go out for a while at noon, and Carole seems to think I shouldn't see you again today before we leave this evening—so I guess the next time I'll see you will be in church.'

Vicki swallowed and managed a faint smile. 'She's insisting that I get dressed over at her house and she wants us to have a drink with them after the church service. I'm going over there this afternoon to help her vacuum and make some canapés.'

He smiled. 'They're good friends.'

'Yes, you're lucky.'

'No, Vicki—*we're* lucky.'

We . . . a small word that could mean so much. She fell silent. She felt the quick touch of his lips on her cheek and heard him say, 'I must get some work done—see you tonight.'

Because Carole kept her busy, the afternoon passed quickly. Perched on stools at the counter, they all ate an early supper, after which Philip shooed the women off to get dressed so he could clean up the kitchen. The guest room had been set aside for Vicki; she had washed her hair that morning, so now she had a quick shower and dressed in her laciest underwear, slipping the soft white dress over her head. Her hair she brushed loose on her shoulders. A touch of mascara and creamy eyeshadow and a pale pink lip gloss completed her preparations. She circled slowly in front of the mirror, watching the diamond at her throat splinter the light into tiny sparks of colour. She was very pale and her eyes looked huge; her hands were ice-cold.

'Ready, Vicki?'

She took a deep breath and opened the door, walking down the hall. Carole was in the kitchen. 'You look lovely, Vicki,' she said warmly.

'I—I'm scared,' Vicki blurted without any finesse. 'I don't even know why I'm marrying him, Carole.'

'Sure you do,' the older woman said comfortably. 'You're marrying him because you love him. Just as I married Philip because I loved him. But on my wedding day when I got to the church, if it hadn't been for my father holding on to my arm, I think I'd have run the other way—it's just nerves. You'll be all right as soon as you see Garth. Which reminds me. . . .' She took a large flat box out of the refrigerator. 'Garth said to give this to you just before you left.'

The surprise that Stephen had talked about . . . Vicki lifted off the lid. Nestled in tissue paper was a small sweet-smelling bouquet of white freesias, with a pale pink orchid as its centre. With exquisite care she lifted it out, and only then did she see the card tucked down the side of the box. In angular, very masculine handwriting that she already recognised was written: 'These flowers reminded me of your sweetness, your purity and your beauty. Garth.'

She swallowed hard, blinking back tears, and wordlessly showed the car to her friend. 'Are you still scared?' Carole said gently.

'Not as much, no.'

'Good. We'd better go—it'll take us twenty minutes to get to the Bay.'

The two boys came in, resplendent in suits and ties, their vivid hair slicked down to unaccustomed tidiness, followed by Philip, unexpectedly handsome in a light grey suit; Carole herself was wearing a very attractive flowered smock. They all got in Philip's station wagon, Vicki carefully protecting her bouquet.

Garth's car was already parked outside the church, and the lights shone bravely into the night from the building's tall pointed windows. The air was cool, although not unpleasantly so, while from the shore came the soft murmur of the waves. Vicki clutched her flowers, not realising that they were shaking in her grip. Philip came over to her and offered her his arm, while Carole followed between the two boys. The steps to the door seemed endless; the lights blinded Vicki and she hesitated in the vestibule, the pulse in her throat beating frantically. Then, at the far end of the aisle, she saw the tall figure of the man who was waiting for her.

As though he sensed her presence he turned, and across the distance that separated them she saw his grave smile and felt his calmness reach to her. The fingers that had been clutching Philip's sleeve with a kind of desperation gradually slackened their hold. She looked up at her escort. 'I'm ready,' she said quietly. 'Shall we go?'

They walked up the aisle to the altar where Philip released her, stepping back. Garth took her free hand and squeezed it gently. He must have felt how cold it was and again he gave her that quiet, steady smile as if there was no one else present but her.

The service began, the ancient, beautiful words flowing sonorously over the small group. Vicki made her responses clearly, held out her hand as Garth slipped a plain gold band on her finger, stood mutely as he kissed her. Then there were forms to sign with her new name, Vicki Travis, and finally it was over. Only seven people there besides herself, and of the seven it was Stephen who was Vicki's first concern. He was standing beside Andrew, obviously rather overawed by the proceedings, and when she spoke to him, he walked up to her stiffly, his eyes as wary as the first time he had seen her. She knelt, putting her hands on his shoulders, her face level with his. 'Well, Stephen,' she said, all her love for him warming her brown eyes, 'you're stuck with me now, I'm afraid.'

His face was very serious. 'You'll be my mother now,

won't you? You won't go away?'

'Yes, I will be—and no, I won't,' she said, answering each question in turn.

The grey eyes, so like his father's, glinted with mischief. 'You'll have to make lots of chocolate cakes.'

'That's a promise, too!' Suddenly they were hugging each other fiercely, and the difficult moment was over. Everyone else crowded around to congratulate her and Garth and when they all finally went outside, Stephen was perfectly content to travel with the Hunters, leaving Vicki and his father to follow in Garth's car. After shutting her door, Garth came around the front of the car and sat beside her. He made no move to start the engine and her smile wavered. Very softly he said, 'I've done it—I've made you my wife, Vicki.'

The quietness with which he spoke did not deceive her; his voice was full of triumph, the blatant triumph of the male who has singled out his mate and now asserts his pride of ownership. Her mind went blank and her fingers tightened around the ribboned clasp of her bouquet.

At random she said, 'The flowers are beautiful—thank you. It must have been difficult to arrange getting them all the way up here.'

He did not even look at the bouquet and she wondered if he had heard her. 'Come here,' he said thickly. 'I want to kiss you.'

A quick glance around and she saw that everyone else had gone, leaving the church in darkness. 'We'd better go. The Hunters will be expecting us——'

'They, of all people, will understand.' He grabbed her by the shoulders, twisting her to face him and as she raised her hands instinctively to ward him off, the bouquet slid unnoticed to the floor. His mouth was rough and bruising, forcing her lips apart. Within her, primitive desire warred with an equally primitive fear. She never knew which would have won, for Garth let her go as precipitately as he had seized her, the triumph blazing in his face now as his eyes roamed over the shining fall of her hair, the softness of her breasts, and the slender length of her thighs under the folds of her white skirt.

Heat enveloped her so that her cheeks flamed with colour, for he might just as well have undressed her, so possessive was his gaze. 'Garth——'

'It's all right—we won't stay long at the Hunters',' he said, completely misunderstanding her plea.

Numbly she watched as he turned the ignition key and the engine roared to life. Her eyes fell to her lap, where the gold ring gleamed on her finger, and only then did she notice the bouquet on the floor of the car. She bent to pick it up. In the dim light from the dashboard she could see that the petals were crushed and bruised and in her over-wrought state it seemed somehow symbolic, a bad omen.

However, when they reached the Hunters' there was the welcoming blaze of lights and inside warmth and laughter and the delicious fragrance of the canapés. A drink was thrust in her hand and rashly Vicki swallowed it down, determined that neither Carole nor Philip should sense her anxiety. Carole was at her most vivacious, so obviously happy about the marriage that Vicki caught some of her friend's lighthearted gaiety; laughing at some quip of Carole's, her cheeks flushed and eyes over-bright, she looked up to find Garth watching her, and recklessly she raised her glass to him, her pose unconsciously provocative.

His eyes holding her mesmerised, he drained his own glass; he had, she thought with a qualm of unease, been drinking steadily since they came. Because Stephen grabbed her sleeve, she turned away, not seeing Garth fill his glass again.

It was after ten when Garth said lightly, tweaking Stephen's ear, 'It's way past your bedtime, son—so I think Vicki and I had better go.' He glanced over at Carole. 'Although I hate to leave a good party.'

She said primly, 'Tonight you're forgiven.'

'We'll try to restrain Stephen from wanting to rush over first thing in the morning,' her husband added.

'Good luck,' Garth said drily. 'Why did I have to have a son who thinks that seven a.m. is the best time of the day?'

No one seemed able to answer that, and under the cover of the ensuing laughter and Stephen's indignant rejoinder, Carole murmured to Vicki, 'Be happy, Vicki dear—you have a fine man. And don't worry, everything will be all right tonight, I know it will.'

So Carole had not been deceived. . . . 'I guess I am a bit nervous,' Vicki admitted.

'That's natural enough—I was scared to death, as I recall! But of course, you've been married before, it's not as though you're the complete innocent I was.' Carole smiled, her eyes tender as they rested on the lanky figure of her husband.

Abruptly Vicki got up. 'That was a lovely party, Carole, thank you.'

'Very good food,' Carole agreed blandly, and they both chuckled.

In a flurry of goodbyes, Vicki and Garth were ushered out of the door. Neither spoke all the way home, Garth apparently concentrating on the winding road, Vicki unable to think of anything to say. They went in through the back door. The house was quiet and empty . . . waiting, the girl thought with a frisson up her spine. As Garth closed and latched the door behind him, the click of the key in the lock sounded very loud.

'I forgot,' he said suddenly, his voice genuinely amused. 'I'm supposed to carry you over the threshold, aren't I? I must have other things on my mind.' She blushed, knowing all too well what he meant by that, and stood frozen to the spot as he approached her. 'I'll carry you to my room instead,' he murmured. 'I'd rather do that anyway.'

'I—I'm too heavy,' she protested weakly.

He removed the bouquet from her fingers and put it carefully on the table, before picking her up in his arms. 'You were saying?'

Vicki lowered her eyes in confusion. Down the hall, past the living room, past her door and Stephen's, to the end door—Garth's. He pushed it open with his foot.

CHAPTER TEN

WALKING to the middle of the room, Garth carefully put Vicki down, although briefly his arms remained around her waist as he rained a shower of tiny kisses on her cheek and throat. 'Mmm . . . nice,' he breathed. 'Just stay right where you are while I light the fire, then we can put the light out.'

Garth's room, like hers, overlooked the ocean and there were the same long drapes; but there the resemblance ended. A fringed oriental rug lay on the floor, intricately patterned in shades of peacock blue and tangerine, while the bedspread, of raw silk, was the same peacock hue; it was these colours, so vivid and sure of themselves, that dominated the room. For the rest there was dark polished mahoghany furniture, an array of exquisite Steuben glass, two mysteriously beautiful Impressionist paintings; it was the room of a complex and sophisticated man, very sure of his own taste.

The fire was crackling in the hearth and Garth got up, going into the adjoining bathroom to wash his hands. When he came back he flung his suit jacket across a chair and unknotted his tie. Insignificant actions, in one sense; yet to the watching girl there was an intimacy in his casual undressing that cried a warning.

She began to edge her way to the door. 'Where are you going?' he said sharply.

'To my own room——'

'No, Vicki.'

'To get my nightdress, that's all.'

'You won't be needing it.' He walked past her and closed the door, flicking off the light switch so the room was illuminated only by the leaping flames. His shadow was thrown on the wall behind him, vast and threatening, and instinctively she backed away.

'Come here,' he said.

There was no escape—it was the moment of truth. 'Garth, there's something I have to tell you——'

'Come here, Vicki.'

Holding herself very straight, she approached him. She had no choice, now.... 'Listen to me. I must tell you that——'

But he was not listening. The lines of his face blurred with desire, he said thickly, 'This isn't the time for talking, Vicki.' With his hands buried in the shining thickness of her hair, he pulled her towards him, tilting her face to his. 'I feel as though I've been waiting for this for ever. From the first moment I saw you, I knew I had to have you.' His mouth found hers and he kissed her with a hunger so elemental that her own needs, starved for so long, leapt to answer his. For a moment fear was forgotten in a kiss that went on and on, enveloping her whole body in the heat that would inevitably kindle desire.

When Garth finally moved back, his chest was rising and falling with his rapid breathing and his grey eyes were smouldering with passion. He knelt at her feet and took off her shoes. Fingers rough with haste, he undid the belt of her dress and then the buttons, pushing it from her shoulders so that it fell to the floor in a crumpled white heap.

'I want to see you naked,' he whispered.

She flushed, then paled. 'I can't. I——' He slid the straps of her slip and bra off her shoulders. 'Let me leave them on,' she begged. 'Please?'

The thin fabric of her slip clung to the smooth line of breast, waist and hip. His eyes roaming over her, he shrugged out of his shirt, and his trousers, like her dress, fell to the floor. He was magnificently proportioned, his broad chest tapering to narrow hips and long, muscular legs, and again she felt that alien leap of desire.

'We've waited long enough, Vicki—I've got to have you,' he said hoarsely. Sweeping her into his arms, he carried her to the bed, pulling back the covers so that she lay on her back on the smooth sheets. Then he was beside her and there was the sound of tearing fabric as her garments were pulled from her body.

She gasped an incoherent protest, trying to cover herself with the sheet, but he stayed her hands, his eyes drinking in the pale gleam of her flesh, all softness and curves. 'You're so beautiful!' he said fiercely. 'And you're mine now—all mine.' His hands were suddenly violent as he gathered her closer. 'I want you to forget you ever belonged to anyone else—I wish to God you never had.'

'Garth—please listen. . . .'

But his head was at her breast, his lips tracing its fullness, and in spite of herself a wave of such sweetness swept over her that her body arched against his in unconscious invitation.

It was all he needed. Fingers and mouth assailed her body. Through a storm of mingled passion and terror that tossed her from shore to shore as helplessly as if she were a bit of wreckage, she felt his nakedness fall on top of her, crushing her, suffocating her, drowning her . . . . she beat at his back with her fists, sobbing in her throat, twisting her hips in a frantic effort to escape.

He mistook her struggle for consent, the writhing of her limbs for a passion as all-consuming as his own. His hips thrust against hers and suddenly there was pain, a piercing agony. Vicki screamed his name, her body rigid with shock.

Everything stopped. In the luxurious room the sound of her cry seemed to echo, shocking and primeval. Garth pulled his weight off her, supporting himself on his palms. His eyes were appalled as they stared down at her huddled figure, for as though to cut off the sound of her own cry, she had thrust her fist in her mouth; her face was paper-white.

'Vicki, I hurt you. In God's name, what did I do?'

She could not bear it. Twisting over on her stomach, she hid her face in the pillow. Hard, bitter sobs burst from her throat, her whole body shuddering as she wept. Dimly she became aware of being held with infinite tenderness, of being rocked back and forth while soothing words fell on her ear, and gradually the storm of weeping abated. Exhausted and limp, she lay still.

'You've got to tell me about it, Vicki.' His voice was very quiet, but suffused with so much gentleness that she found the courage to open her eyes. She rubbed her wet cheeks with the edge of the sheet.

'Yes. It's very simple really,' she said wearily. She raised her eyes to his. 'You see, I'm a virgin, Garth.'

His face blank with shock, he said, 'But, Vicki, you were married for over a year!'

'I know.' Her eyes fell, and she plucked at the sheet. 'It was so humiliating—I've never told anyone before.'

As if he was feeling his way over strange new ground, Garth said carefully, 'You and Barry *never* made love?'

'No.' She swallowed. When she spoke her words came out in a rush. 'I already told you that he married me for my money. He didn't love me at all, although I was so infatuated with him it took me quite a while to see that. We didn't go on a honeymoon because he was too busy at work—at least that was what he said, and I believed him. On our wedding day all his friends came to our apartment afterwards and there was a party.' Her mouth twisted. 'And what a party! It ended about three in the morning, by which time Barry had had so much to drink that two of his friends had to put him to bed. The next night he had an important meeting, he said. There was another party the following night. And so on.'

'Didn't you share a bed?'

'No. When we furnished the apartment he insisted on single beds. He said he slept better alone.'

'I see.' There was a wealth of meaning in Garth's voice.

'It's a pity I didn't, isn't it?'

'You were very young.'

'Yes—in all fairness, I don't think Barry quite realised just how naïve and innocent I was. Anyway, after this kind of behaviour had gone on for a couple of weeks, I was nearly frantic, and there didn't seem to be anyone I could talk to about it. I finally plucked up my courage to confront him and he fobbed me off with some story of not being ready to have children yet and I was so young that we should wait a while. Not knowing any better, I accepted this at face value and thought he was concerned for me.

'Then we went to a cocktail party at Christine Turner's—she was one of the crowd that Barry always went around with. I used to envy her because she was everything I wasn't—beautiful, sophisticated, and elegant. Well . . . I went looking for Barry around midnight because I wanted to go home. He was talking to Harley Connelly, who was a business associate and one of his best friends—he's been out in Vancouver for nearly a year. . . .'

They hadn't seen her. Barry, she immediately realised, had already drunk enough to be at that dangerously expansive stage when he would say or do anything, no matter how indiscreet; his fair skin was flushed, his balance a little unsteady. Harley, who was a suspiciously black-haired bachelor of uncertain age with a vocabulary that had already made Vicki cringe, was waving a glass and a cigar as he spoke. 'It's too bad you had to get married, old man—it's a state I've always avoided like the plague. Although I suppose in your case there are compensations—she's rather a pretty little thing, your Vicki. Although a bit of a prude. I don't think she approves of me at all.'

'I don't expect she does.'

'But it's easy to see she's head over heels in love with you.'

Barry shifted restlessly. 'You try living with that kind of devotion, twenty-four hours a day.'

'At night it might not be all that bad.' Harley paused suggestively.

'She's all yours. Personally she's not my type—a skinny little kid who doesn't know the score? No, thanks.'

'How very interesting,' Harley said smoothly. 'And

what does Christine think of all this?'

'Christine would have my head if she thought I was sleeping with Vicki,' Barry said moodily. 'I wish to God she'd been the one with the money.'

'Life never works out that way, does it? Too bad, old man.'

'Damn right it's too bad. The only way I could get my hands on the money was to marry Vicki—and now I'm stuck with her.'

'Never mind—at least you got some financial compensation out of marriage. Lots of people don't even get that. By the way, did you hear the latest about Lana and that Italian she's been dating?'

Sick and trembling, Vicki must have made a move, because Barry had turned so quickly that he slopped some of his drink down the front of his immaculate suit. 'Vicki! What do you want?'

An ice-cold calm had settled over her. 'I want you to explain what I just overheard.'

Harley melted discreetly into the background as Barry blustered, 'What are you talking about?'

'You know perfectly well—I want to know why you married me, what Christine has to do with you, why you won't sleep with me!'

'Be quiet!' he hissed. 'Do you want everyone to hear you?'

'I couldn't care less—they probably know anyway.'

She saw by his guilty look that she had hit upon the truth. 'She's your mistress, isn't she?' she said with the calm of despair. 'The only reason you married me is because I inherited all that money.'

He looked her up and down with an ugly sneer. 'I can't imagine why else I'd have married you.'

A minute ago she had thought nothing more could ever hurt her—now she knew differently, for his ugly words seared her like a hot iron. She had failed as a woman. She was so undesirable, so unattractive, that Barry had not even been tempted to make love to her. 'I'm going home,' she said stonily. 'You can do what you like—you're good at that, after all.'

'Stop making such a fuss!' he snapped.

'A fuss?' Her laugh bordered on hysteria. 'You don't even begin to understand what you've done to me, do you, Barry? You're so totally selfish you don't even realise other people have feelings. How could I have been so blind as to fall in love with you? And so stupid as to believe you when you said you loved me—you don't know the meaning of the word.'

He muttered an obscenity uner his breath, grinding his cigarette out in the ashtray. 'I'm going to get another drink.'

She had gone home in a taxi, cried herself into a stupor of exhaustion and finally fallen asleep. . . .

With a start Vicki came back to the present, to the fireshadows dancing on the wall and to Garth's embrace offering her its mute comfort. She said baldly, 'When I overheard Barry talking to Harley, everything I'd been too stupid to see fell into place; he'd married me for my money, he found me totally undesirable, and besides, he already had a mistress—this Christine I mentioned to you. So that was that.' Her mouth twisted cynically. 'The end of love's young dream.'

'What happened then?' Although his voice was under control, there was raw anger burning in Garth's eyes, an anger she knew was on her behalf and which she found strangely comforting.

'Nothing. Things went on much as they had before, except that now I didn't bother going with him to any of the parties and dinners and what have you. As for the money, he was a step ahead of me there—he took most of it out of our joint account and I never did find out what he did with it. Spent it on Christine, most likely.'

Garth was pursuing his own train of thought. 'So he never laid a finger on you?' She hesitated just a split second too long. 'Or did he?' His voice was knife-sharp.

'Only once,' she replied, her slim fingers twisting the

gold chain around her neck, her eyes avoiding his.

'You'd better tell me about that, too,' Garth said grimly.

'Nothing really happened——'

'Tell me.'

There was no disobeying that note in his voice. 'It was a month or so before he was killed. He came home one night earlier than I'd expected. I was just getting out of the shower—I only had a towel around me. He——' she shivered reminiscently, her brown eyes full of a remembered terror.

'He tried to rape you.'

Grateful that she did not have to put it into words, she nodded. 'It was horrible—I was so frightened. But by one of those ironies of fate, Christine phoned before he—anyway, she phoned. While Barry was talking to her, I got dressed and left the apartment and went to a hotel.'

'Did you ever go back to the apartment?'

'Oh, yes—I had to, I couldn't afford to stay in a hotel indefinitely. But I told Barry if he ever tried anything like that again, I'd tell the president of the company why my husband had needed a large sum of money a year ago. Barry knew all too well that an investigation would finish him—so I was safe enough.'

She lay still. Drained by her confession, she felt a strange kind of peace steal over her; sharing those memories had robbed them of some of their power.

Garth stroked a strand of hair back from her cheeks. 'I'm so sorry that I hurt you—it never occurred to me that you hadn't made love before. I wish you'd told me.'

'I tried, don't you remember?'

'You mean when we came into the room a while ago? That's what you were trying to tell me?'

'Yes. But you're quite right, I should have told you sooner. It just seemed so—embarrassing, I guess I didn't have the courage.'

'Do you know why I wouldn't listen to you?'

There was such strained intensity in his voice that she

looked up, shaking her head in bewilderment.

'I was eaten up with jealousy of Barry—a dead man,' he said with savage self-contempt. 'He'd been your husband and as such I assumed he'd known your body in all the intimacies of marriage. When we got here tonight all I could think of was imprinting myself on you, making myself more real to you than he'd ever been, so you'd forget he'd existed. While all the time you'd never truly been his wife. And so I hurt you. . . .'

In swift compassion she reached out and laid a hand against his cheek, wanting to erase the torment from his eyes. 'Garth, it's all right. Please don't look like that. You had no way of knowing. . . .'

He pressed his lips into her palm, his dark head bent. For Vicki all the barriers were down; Garth knew all there was to know about her now—her lack of self-confidence, her fears and inhibitions, the shameful story of her marriage that had not been a marriage. She had bared her soul to him. And now as she lay naked in the shelter of his arms, she knew she was ready to be guided into that other intimacy, the joining of two bodies, the final consummation with the man she loved. She was suddenly achingly conscious of a host of sensations: his thigh heavy against hers; the clean scent of his skin; the weight of his arm across her breast. She closed her eyes, trying to cement that moment of closeness into her memory for all time.

'You look exhausted,' she heard Garth say. She opened her eyes just as he traced a finger under her lashes where the skin was blue-shadowed with fatigue. 'Where do you keep your nightdress?'

'Under the pillow on my bed,' she said uncertainly. He slid his arm free of her and got up, belting his dark blue robe around him as he left the room. When he came back he was carrying her nightdress over his arm. 'Sit up,' he said in a businesslike manner.

She did not want to put on her nightdress; she wanted instead to be held and kissed and caressed. But how could she say that? Her brown eyes filled with confusion she sat up as he slipped the gown over her head.

'Don't look so worried,' he said softly. 'I want you to lie down and go to sleep. You've had more than enough for one day, it's no wonder you look so tired.'

'Where will you be?'

'I'll stay here with you. Now lie down.'

Vicki lay back, her hair dark on the pillow. Garth leaned over and kissed her cheek; it was a kiss a brother could have given, she thought with a sharp pang of disappointment, as he went over to the fireplace to add another log. She *was* tired, desperately tired, but overriding that tiredness and mingling with her disappointment was an almost superstitious fear: this had happened before.

She did not want to sleep alone; she wanted Garth beside her. Forgetting her pride, desperate to eradicate the ghosts of the past, she looked over at Garth. He had settled himself in an armchair by the fire, a book open on his lap; for him, the matter was plainly closed. Her courage failed her. Perhaps for reasons of his own he did not want to make love to her now. Turning her face to the pillow, lying very still, she eventually fell asleep.

Sunlight streaming across the bed awoke her the next morning. An unfamiliar room, an unfamiliar bed ... memory rushed back and she searched the room quickly with her eyes. No sign of Garth; the door was partly ajar, so he must already have dressed and gone out. The gold bedside clock said nine-twenty; she had slept for hours.

About to sit up, she heard the sound of voices coming down the hall, and hurriedly pulled the covers up to her chin. 'Vicki sleeps in your room now?' she heard Stephen ask.

'Yes—now that we're married, she does. Why don't you knock on the door in case she's still asleep?'

A tap on the door. 'Come in,' said Vicki. 'Hi, Stephen. How are you today?'

'I'm fine. We brought you tea.'

The three of them sat companionably on the bed while Stephen described the cartoons he had seen on television early that morning. The tenor for the day was set: a leisurely day spent as a family. They worked in the garden;

all three helped with the meals; in the afternoon they took Garth's boat along the shore to a cave where the crumbling cliffs sometimes exposed fossils. The sun danced on the water and the seabirds swooped white and grey against the brilliant sky. At the wheel Garth stood with legs straddled, the wind ruffling his hair, his hand on Stephen's shoulder as he explained the workings of the depth-sounder. Watching the wake bubble and froth at the stern, Vicki knew she should have been perfectly happy, for she was with the two people she loved most in the world. But she was conscious of a growing sense of unease. Ever since she had told Garth the true story of her marriage, he had been comforting, gentle, kind— which was all very well, but it was hardly the kind of behaviour one would expect from the man of passion that she knew him to be. Today, the first day of their married life, he had not kissed her; beyond helping her into the boat, he had not even touched her. He was as far removed from the lover of last night as he could be. Why? She wished she knew. And what would happen tonight? She wished she knew that, too. All the old doubts and uncertainties that Barry had played upon so skilfully rose up to mock her, poisoning the beauty of the sea and sky and stealing the joy that should have been hers.

The slow hours marched on. Home again. Supper. A game of cards with Stephen before he was put to bed. Then Garth and Vicki walked back into the living room where they had been sitting around the fire, and Garth threw on another log. 'I suppose we should wait a few minutes and give him time to get to sleep, before we go to bed ourselves,' he said calmly, settling himself in his chair and opening the notebook she knew he used as a journal.

She sat quietly across from him, a book open on her lap, her eyes fastened instead on the incandescent heart of the fire where the gold and orange light pulsed with a life of its own. Her throat was tight with panic and her fingers were cold; she envied Garth his air of concentration as much as she feared it, for it seemed to epitomise his lack of concern about the night to come.

Finally he capped his pen, tucking it in the notebook as a marker. Getting up, he stretched as lazily as a mountain cat. 'Ready, Vicki?'

She carefully closed her book, which was at the same page it had been an hour ago, and stood up. She was still wearing the jeans and heavy gold sweater she had worn on the boat, an outfit that gave her a slim boyishness, although above the sweater her curved mouth and gold-flecked eyes were totally feminine. Her face was very pale, the set of her lips wary and uncertain.

Garth looked at her sharply. 'Are you all right?'

'Of course,' she said coolly. 'You'd better put the screen in front of the fire, hadn't you?'

'Yes . . . did you enjoy yourself today?'

'The sea was beautiful,' she said evasively.

He stepped closer and his hand clamped on her shoulder. 'That's not what I asked. Did you like being with us—did you feel like one of the family?'

Puzzled, she said, 'Oh yes—you know I always enjoy being with Stephen.'

His mouth thinned to an ugly line. 'It's always Stephen with you, isn't it, Vicki?'

'I don't know what you mean.'

'Is that hy you married me, so you could always be with Stephen?'

'I like being with you, too,' she said weakly.

'Thanks,' he jeered. 'Thanks a lot!'

'Please, Garth——'

'Why *did* you marry me, Vicki?'

That was the one secret she could not share with him. 'This is ridiculous, Garth!' she said furiously.

'Answer me.' His fingers tightened cruelly on her shoulder.

Struggling to free herself, she seethed, 'Let go! You know why I married you, Garth Travis—as I recall, you threatened to get rid of me if I didn't. You used my attachment for Stephen as a weapon over me—or have you conveniently forgotten that?'

He stopped her torrent of words with his mouth. A

brutal kiss, punishing in its intensity, his arms around her like iron bars. She could have shrunk from him and struggled to be free. But anger had liberated her from fear, and her response, fuelled by a day of frustration, was as fierce as his demand. Her arms encircled his neck, pulling his head closer and her fingers tangled themselves in his hair. Her body, pliant as flame, made a mockery of his strength, for she was a willing prisoner with no desire to escape.

They broke apart by a kind of mutual, unspoken consent. His chest was heaving, his eyes smoke-grey to the molten gold of hers. 'Vicki——' he began heavily.

On the desk in the hall the telephone shrilled. 'Who in hell's that at this hour of the night?' Garth said irritably. 'I won't be a minute—don't go away.'

As if she would, she thought with a kind of desperate humour. Each of her senses was clamouring for his touch, and although her response to his kiss faintly horrified her in retrospect, she knew it had been inevitable—and would, given the chance, happen again. She sat down on the edge of the hearth, unable to avoid hearing his voice from the hall.

'Hello?' A long silence. 'Of course I will, Philip. . . . Sure, I'll be right over. . . . Don't apologise, man, you'd do the same for me. Be there in five minutes.'

The receiver banged back on the telephone and Garth strode into the living room. 'That was Philip—Carole's having labour pains and the doctor thinks she should go to the hospital. So Phil wants one of us to stay with the boys. I'd better go over there and you stay here—okay?'

Vicki's face was concerned as she nodded her consent. 'I do hope she'll be all right. Give her my love, Garth, won't you?'

He checked momentarily as though about to say something, then said evenly, 'Lock the door behind me, will you? I have a key.'

She followed him through the kitchen to the back door, where he turned to face her. 'We'll continue our discussion when I get back,' he said, a threat implicit in the quietly spoken words. 'Sleep well.'

Unconsciously she stepped back a pace. 'I'm not sure there's anything to discuss. For whatever our separate reasons, we *are* married—it's a bit late to be wrangling over motives.'

'I disagree. However, it will keep.' His eyes raked her figure from head to toe. 'Sleep well—because the other thing we have to continue when I get back is that kiss.'

The door snapped shut behind him and she flicked the lock, wishing she could as easily lock away her heart and body from his invasion, and knowing, even as she thought it, how impossible it was. Through the window she saw the diminishing gleam of his headlights and watched until he was out of sight. A few minutes later Philip's station wagon drove past and with it she sent a quick prayer for Carole and her unborn child. Then, without even thinking, she went to the familiarity of her own room and fell into bed.

The next day she was awoken by the alarm, an unusual occurrence, for Stephen had his own built-in alarm, earlier than anyone else's, and almost always woke her in the morning. When she went to his room, he was drowsy and listless, his forehead warm and his cheeks flushed—he probably had a touch of the 'flu that had been going through the school, she decided, bringing him juice and an aspirin. He was soon asleep again and she was seated at the kitchen table finishing her breakfast when she heard Garth's car come up the driveway. As he walked in the door, there was a mute question in her eyes.

'False alarm,' he said briefly. 'The pains stopped around two in the morning, so Philip brought her home again.' He gave a reluctant grin. 'Carole, being Carole, is hopping mad!'

'Oh, dear, I'm sure she is,' Vicki commiserated. 'Surely that means it won't be long, though.'

'I don't know—the doctor seems to think it could be another couple of weeks.'

'Sit down and I'll get you some breakfast,' she said, setting another place at the table. 'I kept Stephen home today, he has a bit of a temperature.'

'Oh? I'll go and have a look at him. I'll have a quick shower too, I didn't sleep very well last night and it might wake me up.'

She sectioned half a grapefruit and made fluffy scrambled eggs. When Garth came back, he still looked very tired and had apparently forgotten his threats of the night before, for he filled in the details of Carole's hospital visit as he ate and then got up. 'I'd better try and get some work done. I'll see you at lunchtime.'

The hours dragged by. Vicki tried to work on her own book, but without much success; she thought of visiting Carole, but doubted her ability to disguise her inner uncertainty and confusion, and she knew at this point she certainly couldn't unload her troubles on Carole. Stephen slept most of the day, but by late afternoon it was obvious he was on the mend, beginning to recover both his appetite and his normal exuberance. However, there were none of his usual protests at bedtime and by nine o'clock he was sound asleep again.

Vicki and Garth tiptoed out of his room, Garth closing the door quietly behind him. Vicki was about to go to the living room when Garth's hand closed around her arm. She frowned slightly, feeling the old panic strum along her nerves. 'Don't—you're hurting!'

His grip slackened infinitesimally. 'We'll go to my room now.'

'But it's early—only nine o'clock.'

'Good—that gives us all the longer.' Inexorably he began steering her down the hallway.

This time fear conquered anger and she let herself be led into his room. The door shut and he turned her to face him. She stared at one of the buttons on his shirt, her heartbeat threatening to choke her.

When he spoke there was reluctant concern in his voice. 'You look tired.'

Her nerves on edge, she snapped, 'That's just another way of telling a woman she looks unattractive, isn't it?'

'Don't be silly——'

'Well, I *am* tired. So why don't you let me sleep in my room?'

'This is your room now. Although I noticed you didn't sleep here last night—you're not going to make a habit of that, Vicki.'

All the accumulated tension of the past forty-eight hours exploded within her and her laugh had more than a touch of hysteria. 'I don't see that it makes much difference. We've been married for two days—married but not married. In theory I'm your wife—but I'm not really, am I, Garth?' Now that she had started, she couldn't stop, although a tiny part of her brain was horrified by her unbridled tongue. '*We* know I'm not your wife, don't we? It's just like last time. . . .'

He shook her. 'Stop it, Vicki! You know it's not like last time.'

'Oh, yes, it is—every night there was an excuse. . . .'

'We've only spent one night together and you were exhausted. Last night couldn't be helped—was I supposed to say no to Philip?'

Her breath caught in a sob. 'No, you couldn't do that. But Barry always had the perfect excuse——'

'I'm not Barry! And the sooner you get that through your head, the better.'

She knew he was speaking the simple truth; she had been a fool to ever compare them. She began to shiver. Her head drooped forward so that her hair hid her face. 'I'm sorry. It's just so horribly repetitive. It frightens me.'

Garth held her close. 'I'm sorry, too—I shouldn't have lost my temper. The last two days have seemed endless to me—wanting you and yet not able to have you——'

She interrupted, knowing that for the sake of her own sanity she had to have the truth. 'You really do want me, Garth?'

He gazed into her eyes, his own desperately serious. 'I want you more than I've ever wanted a woman before. You're all the beauty and all the passion I shall ever need.'

If she could not believe him now, then she could not believe anything. The tremors that had shaken her died away. She held herself still—still and waiting.

With a hand that was not quite steady, he traced the delicate line of her cheek, the softness of her lips. 'So beautiful. . . .' he whispered. 'Vicki, I know this is the first time for you and I'll be as gentle as I can—will you trust me?'

She brought her hands up to rest on his shoulders, her fingers kneading his flesh through the thin shirt. Sensing that it was he who now needed reassurance, she said with all the generosity of her nature, 'Yes, Garth, I trust you.' As though sealing a pledge, she reached up and kissed his mouth with an entrancing blend of shyness and audacity. She felt his shudder of desire, felt his arms tighten around her as his lips took the initiative from hers, probing, questing, exploring.

Reluctantly they drew apart, the rapid sound of their breathing mingling in the quiet of the night. Garth began to undo her blouse and slid it from her shoulders. Wanting only to please him, Vicki fumbled with the buttons of his shirt, her fingers brushing his skin. Closing her eyes she ran her fingertips up his body from navel to collarbone. Bone and muscles and hair-rough skin, she wanted to know every inch of him. . . .

Skirt and lingerie joined the heap of clothes on the floor. He gathered her naked body in his arms and carried her to the bed. And there, encouraging her every need, eliciting in her a slow gathering of wave after wave of pleasure, he guided her through the turbulent waters of passion unfulfilled to the very heart of the storm where their voices soared like the seabirds' and amidst shafts of white light they broke through to shared ecstasy and peace.

Her eyes still dark with wonderment, Vicki lay still, her hair tossed on the pillow like seaweed in foam. She had journeyed a long way. Yet because of her companion's tenderness and care, she had felt not fear but joy. Because of him she was for the first time in her life truly a woman.

He was leaning on one elbow watching her and she

knew she must try and share this with him. 'Garth?' she said tentatively.

'Yes, dear?' He held a strand of her hair to his lips, inhaling its sweet scent.

He was not a man for easy endearments and unconsciously her lips curved, the smile reflected in her eyes. She laid a hand across the taut arc of his ribs.

'Garth, I want to say this now, and then I think it should be forgotten. I'm glad I never made love with Barry. I'm glad it was you who——' her cheeks flushed pink, she stumbled to a halt. 'You were so good to me,' she rushed on, a sheen of tears in her eyes. 'Thank you.'

He kissed her gently, lingeringly. 'You're more than I deserve, Vicki—so generous, recklessly giving everything you have.' He hesitated, his eyes momentarily bleak as he lost himself in memories of a long-ago past. 'I don't talk much about Stephen's mother—Corinne. I don't want to. But I do want you to know that tonight was unique for me, too. I think it was as important, if not more so, for you to give me pleasure as to receive it—I've never experienced that before, Vicki. So it's my turn to thank you.'

He settled himself beside her, holding her close, and it was with the sound of his breathing in her ear and the warmth of his body against hers that she fell asleep.

She woke in the night to a hand rhythmically stroking her thighs, filling her with the ache of desire. Bolder now, she guided his mouth to her breasts, feeling her flesh swell, her nipples harden to his touch. Fiercely he held her and just as fiercely she arched her body to his, exulting in his hardness as his weight crushed her to the bed. There was no need for words this time, no need for gentleness; each knew what the other wanted, and as Garth found his release in her she raked her fingernails down his spine, drowning, drowning, drowning until he and she were one and there was nothing else in the world. . . .

CHAPTER ELEVEN

When Vicki woke next, it was to the sound of a tentative tapping at the door. 'Dad? Vicki? No one got me up for school.'

Garth's head had been lying on her breast, her arms holding him close even in sleep. He grinned at her lazily as he pulled the covers over her nakedness. 'Come in, Stephen.'

'It's nine o'clock,' the little boy announced. 'How come we all slept so late?'

'I can't imagine,' Garth murmured, a wicked glint in his eye.

Vicki said firmly, 'I expect you overslept because you were getting over the 'flu, Stevie. How are you feeling?'

'Fine.' He cocked his head hopefully. 'Do I get to stay home today?'

'I think you'd better if you had a temperature yesterday,' his father said.

'Yippee! I can play with my race cars.' About to rush out of the room, Stephen stopped, looking down at the foot of the bed, and said gleefully, 'Dad, you're always hollering at me if I leave my clothes lying around on the floor—why are you doing it now?'

For once Vicki saw Garth at a loss for words. Fortunately Stephen didn't wait for a reply and as he ran down the hallway, making a noise like a race car revving up, she began to laugh helplessly.

'Are you laughing at me?' Garth demanded, tickling her ribs until she squealed for mercy. 'It's your clothes as well, you know.' He buried his face in her neck, nibbling at her skin. 'I wish we could stay here all day. But I suppose we'd better get up.'

One last, hard kiss and he untangled himself from the sheets and stood up. Vicki lay back, admiring the long lines of his body, so intimately known to her in the dark hours of the night. As though he felt her eyes on him, he looked down, seeing the tumbled hair, the faint blue shadows under her eyes, the sensuous fullness of her lips. 'If you keep looking like that, I'll never be able to leave your bed,' he said, and between them, openly acknowledged in the bright morning light, lay all the passion and delight they had shared.

She said demurely, 'I'd advise a cold shower.'

He threw back his head and laughed. It was so vital and youthful a sound that she felt her heart contract with love for him and she almost missed his next words. 'Do something for me?' he asked. 'Wear the caftan that Carole gave you this morning? But nothing else . . . Stephen won't know the difference, but I will.'

As he disappeared into the bathroom, she stretched sensuously, knowing she had never been so happy in her life before. It did not seem to matter that he had not told her he loved her; his every action, his care for her, both physically and emotionally, spoke of love more clearly than any words. Humming softly to herself, she got up and went to her old room, where she showered quickly before pulling the rich folds of the caftan over her head. Catching a glimpse of herself in the mirror, she smiled, knowing that never again would she doubt that Garth found her beautiful.

In the kitchen Stephen bolted down his cereal so that he could go back to the playroom, where he had a complicated system of plastic tracks set up for his racing car. Garth and Vicki stayed at the table sipping their coffee, an ease and warmth between them that delighted the girl.

'You're going to have to lock me in the study today,' he yawned. 'How's your book going, Vicki, by the way?'

'Slowly!'

He grinned at her. 'Self-discipline, woman, that's what you need.' He poured himself more coffee. 'Look at me—a perfect example of it!'

She gazed up at the ceiling. 'You can have your

choice—I could work on chapter five today, or I could cook roast beef with all the trimmings and a deep dish apple pie.'

'You're appealing to the worst in me.' He let his eyes fall deliberately to the deep 'V' of her neckline. 'Well, almost the worst.'

Blushing, she got up to make herself a piece of toast. 'Oh, someone's coming—Phil and Carole,' she said, watching the station wagon come up the slope. 'I hope nothing's wrong.'

Carole soon dispelled this concern. 'I'm fine,' she said. 'Darn it!'

Vicki rinsed out the percolator to make fresh coffee, reaching for the canister at the same time as Garth stretched across for more spoons. They collided, his arms swiftly encircling her, and briefly she leaned against him in a movement of surrender far more revealing than she realised.

Carole was watching them. '*You* certainly look fine, Vicki,' she said roundly. 'Married life agrees with you.'

Vicki could no more have stopped the tide of colour that rose in her face than she could have stopped breathing. 'Oh—thanks,' she murmured, looking anywhere but at Garth.

Amused by her confusion, Garth said, 'What about me? Don't I get any compliments?'

'You look very much as Phil did two days after we were married,' Carole teased. 'Haggard, circles under your eyes—in other words, short on sleep.'

'As I recall,' Philip interposed, 'it was you who wouldn't let me get any sleep.'

'Touché,' his wife giggled. 'Did you make those muffins, Vicki? I shouldn't have one, but may I?'

Happiness, Vicki thought—such an elusive quality, so difficult to imagine when you were without it, so blindingly beautiful when it was yours. She carried it with her all that day and far into the night like a golden banner. As the firelight flickered on the ceiling and the shadows danced on the walls of their bedroom, she and Garth made love again, and she was like tinder burning to his flame. Afterwards she slept in his arms; they seemed a haven from any storm the world could send her.

Stephen went back to school the next day. Vicki spent the morning pottering around the house, moving her clothes into Garth's room, baking a cake, sketching some new ideas she had had for her book. After lunch Garth went back to his study, albeit reluctantly, because he was expecting a call from his Toronto publisher; although it had rained that morning, the sky had cleared by noon and Vicki decided to go for a walk. She set off down the road that wound along the cliff's edge, her hands thrust in her pockets, the wind tossing her hair. Far below the waves fretted at the rocks, while above the treetops herring gulls swooped and soared on invisible air currents. Breathing deeply of the ocean's tang, she felt glad to be alive and her step was buoyant as she topped the hill.

A truck was slowly climbing up the steep slope towards her, its engine grinding. Nils's truck . . . delighted to see her ld friend, she waved her hand, a wide smile on her face, stepping to the edge of the road as he reached her.

'Hi, Nils!' she cried as he wound down the window. 'I haven't seen you for ages—I expected you long before this.'

He grinned at her, the wind ruffling his flaxen hair. 'Been busy,' he said economically. 'Good lobster season, though.'

'And that's hard work, isn't it?' she said sympathetically. 'Here, I'll hop in the truck and we'll go up to the house. You'll stay for supper, won't you?'

'Maybe we'd better not go up to the house right away,' he said slowly. 'I have something to tell you.'

'And I have something to tell *you*!'

But he was already staring down at her left hand with its tell-tale gold band and under his tan his face was suddenly pale. 'Where'd you get that ring?'

Vicki had hoped that in the intervening weeks he had forgotten his hasty proposal of marriage. But as he gazed at her, blue eyes aghast, she knew she had been wrong.

Oh damn. . . . 'I was married four days ago, Nils,' she said apologetically.

'Who'd you marry?'

'Garth, of course.' Who else?

'God, Vicki, what did you do that for?'

He, of anyone, deserved the truth. 'I fell in love with him,' she said simply. 'Nils, I'm sorry—I didn't realise you'd mind so much. I guess I assumed since I hadn't heard from you that perhaps you'd met someone else—or at least had forgotten me. And we only had a very small wedding; just two friends as witnesses and the three boys. No other guests.'

Nils did not seem to have heard a word she said. 'You better get in,' he said roughly.

She went around the hood of the truck to the other side, clambering up into the high seat. Nils's face was set and grim and unconsciously he was banging his knuckles on the wheel with a restrained violence that frightened her. 'I'm sorry,' she repeated miserably. 'I didn't realise you'd take it so badly.'

'It's bad all right. But not just for the reasons you think.' Checking in the mirror, he backed the truck across a culvert and turned down the hill. 'We'll go up here a way and park by the beach so we can talk.'

'But what about?' she demanded, her voice sharp with an anxiety she could no longer deny.

'You'll see.'

There was no moving him when he used that tone of voice, she knew. The truck bounded down the hill, then Nils took a little-used track to the left that led to a deserted wharf and fish shack, the weathered boards as grey as the sea and sad with the sadness of all things abandoned. The waves tumbled untidily on the shore, rattling the stones in their retreat.

Looking straight ahead of him at the distant horizon with his far-seeing fisherman's eyes, Nils said, 'You remember I told you that I'd heard something about Garth Travis, only I couldn't remember what?' She nodded wordlessly, a premonition of disaster brushing her like the wings of a wind-borne raven. 'Well, after you left to come here, I got to worrying about it. So one day I took the day off and went to the city library and looked up his name in the reference section where they keep all the old newspapers and magazines. And I found what I'd been looking for.' For the first time he looked directly at her, his mouth twisted. 'That was a week ago. If only I'd come then, you'd never have married him. But I didn't think there was any hurry and I'd already missed a day's fishing.'

Her voice seemed to have failed her. She fought down an irrational surge of panic. 'What did you find?' she faltered.

'The man's no good, Vicki, an out-and-out bastard. You might as well say he drove his wife to her death—it's little wonder the brother came back looking for revenge.'

Harold ... she had almost forgotten about him. Corinne's brother, who had hated Garth enough to take away his son. She seized Nils by the sleeve, her fingers digging into his arm. 'Garth's *not* like that!' she cried. 'He's a good man, I know he is!'

There was no answering anger in Nils, only pity in the pale blue eyes, and that frightened her more than anything else could have. She took a deep breath. 'Nils, you must tell me what he's supposed to have done.'

He reached down into the pocket in the door of the truck and extracted a cardboard folder. 'They wouldn't let me take the newspapers out of the library, so I had the stuff photocopied,' he said. 'It's all in order.' Not looking at her, he placed the folder in her lap.

She opened it. A newspaper photograph stared up at her: Garth in evening clothes, tall and debonair, on her arm an exquisitely beautiful woman, sloe-eyed and slender, wrapped in luxurious furs. The caption read, 'Author Paul Tarrant and his wife, well-known actress Corinne Lingard, arrive together for the premiere of her latest film. This joint appearance allayed rumours of an impending separation.'

Vicki did not want to read the article below the caption.

The next page, apparently from a movie magazine, was a close-up of Corinne, and not even the poor quality of the print could dim her vital beauty, her engaging smile. 'Corinne Lingard was escorted to the O'Keefe Centre last night by American film director Stanislaus Protsky. The widowed Mr Protsky has been seen frequently in Miss Lingard's company of late. Husband Paul Tarrant's only comment: No comment.'

A photo of Corinne with a younger Stephen, on Corinne's face an expression of gravity, of inner suffering bravely borne. 'Actress Corinne Lingard has formally separated from her husband of seven years, author Paul Tarrant. Shown above with her son Stephen, Miss Lingard is quoted as saying, "My husband and I have agreed it is in our best interests and those of our son that we part. Stephen will, of course, be living with me. I shall be taking a temporary rest from film-making in order to spend as much time as possible with him." Mr Tarrant, who is in London visiting the British representatives of his publishing house, was not available for comment.'

The next, a tersely phrased newspaper article, its head-lines, 'Actress Accuses Husband of Kidnapping Son.' Briefly Vicki closed her eyes, feeling a lightness in her head, a roaring in her ears. Her face was pale as she skimmed through the close-written paragraph. Garth had apparently returned from Britain, removed Stephen bodily from Corinne's apartment and taken him to his own house. For reporters, again that enigmatic 'No comment.'

Piteous, appealing, Corinne's eyes gazed up into Vicki's from a face stripped to a tragic mask. 'Famous actress distraught. Longs for her son. "Stephen needs a mother's love and only I can give him that."'

Article after article. Public support grows for actress Corinne Lingard. Author Paul Tarrant booed by crowds gathered outside his Toronto home. Refuses access to wife. Court case inevitable. Date set for custody battle. Corinne Lingard seen with her constant companion Stanislaus Protsky, who has been quoted as saying, 'Of course Miss

Lingard will win this case. Stephen belongs with his mother.' A photograph of Garth leaving a restaurant alone, his face grim with suppressed anger. 'Television appeal by actress Corinne Lingard moves thousands of watchers.'

Then, finally, the glaring black headlines: 'Actress Corinne Lingard Killed in Plane Crash. Miss Lingard, an accomplished pilot who has had her licence for over ten years, was killed yesterday when flying her ex-husband's four-seater craft from Winnipeg to Toronto. An investigation will be launched into the cause of the crash. Miss Lingard was due to appear in court on Wednesday to plead for custody of her only son, Stephen, removed from her domicile by her ex-husband, writer Paul Tarrant, two months ago.'

A more flamboyant, less cautious periodical blared: 'Actress killed in husband's plane before court case. Son will stay with father now.'

The last page. 'Funeral of Corinne Lingard mobbed by angry crowds.' A shot of Garth in an unguarded moment, his face a rictus of uncontrollable fury as he shoved his way towards the funeral car.

Dazed, Vicki closed the folder, her mind in a tumult. Nils had been waiting for her to finish. 'You see what I mean?' he said grimly.

She was still fighting to take it all in. Her face blank with shock, she sifted through the collection of articles again, searching for a loophole, a way out. But the evidence was damning. Garth had taken Stephen away from Corinne, refused to allow her to even see him. And then, before it could be settled legally, Corinne had been killed—in Garth's plane. From a long way back she had a memory of Garth gripping her arm, saying, 'I didn't murder her, you know.' Had he been lying to her, even then?

But why would he have done it? For it had earned him nothing but censure and abuse. The answer clicked into her brain. Because he had still loved Corinne. He had not wanted her to leave him. And when she had, he had taken the only means of vengeance at hand, and taken Stephen away from her. What other reason could he have had?

In the light of this, Harold's abortive kidnapping attempt had a crude kind of justice. An eye for an eye. Poor Harold, thousands of miles away from the sister he adored at the time when she had needed him most—who could blame him for taking what revenge he could?

She said dully, 'I don't understand why I never heard of any of this before. It was obviously all over the newspapers.'

'Perhaps because they refer to Garth as Paul Tarrant. So you wouldn't have made the connection.'

'But the photographs——' She opened the folder again and her eyes fell on the date—January of last year. Barry had been killed in January. And after his death she had been so ridden with guilt, and so beset by debts and bills and creditors, that the world could have been coming to an end around her and she would not have noticed. . . .

'I wish to God I'd come to see you as soon as I had all this stuff,' Nils repeated, his voice harsh with self-blame. 'You wouldn't have married him then, would you?'

'No,' she said slowly, 'I don't suppose I would.'

'What'll you do now?'

The confines of the truck suddenly seemed claustrophobic. 'Let's walk along the beach,' she said abruptly.

Their footsteps crunched on the shale, a litter of shell fragments and detritus, the tiny skeletons of long-dead sea creatures. The girl scuffed at a pile of rank-smelling seaweed cast up by the tide. She felt very cold. Nils's question was still echoing in her ears and it was still just as unanswerable. What *would* she do now?

Legs apart, she braced herself against the wind; it, at least, was real. The Garth she had fallen in love with, the man who had for the last two nights brought her to the peaks of ecstasy and happiness—was he real? His steadiness, his strength, his humour . . . were they all figments of her imagination, disguising the real Garth: ruthless, implacable, incredibly cruel? And what of his love for

Stephen? That, surely, could not be doubted, any more than could Stephen's love for his father.

'It can't be true!' she burst out. 'Stephen and Garth love each other, I know they do. You can't fake that kind of thing day after day, it's impossible.'

'Nobody ever claimed he didn't love his son,' said Nils with crushing logic. 'As for Stephen, he would only have been four or five at the time, wouldn't he? He probably didn't even know what was going on.'

'What will I *do*?' Her desperate appeal was flung away on the wind.

'If I were you, I'd get out of there as fast as I could. Cut my losses.'

'Nils, I can't!'

'How can you be in love with a guy who did something like he did? These articles couldn't come right out and say it—they'd be sued for libel—but it was pretty obvious they thought there was more to that plane crash than meets the eye.'

She shook her head in frantic denial. 'It's not just Garth, though—there's Stephen. I promised Stephen I'd never leave him. He looks on me as a mother. . . .' Her voice trailed away as she remembered his real mother, the beautiful, doomed Corinne.

'Better to go now than in a year's time. He'll get over it—kids are tough.'

Again she shook her head. 'I couldn't do that to him. I'd never be able to live with myself afterwards.' A wave, sleek and smooth, curled over a rock and disintegrated into a tumble of foam. 'I'll have to go back there, Nils, and somehow have it out with Garth.' A wild hope irradiated her face. 'Maybe there's something we don't know—something the newspapers didn't know or couldn't print.'

'I don't think so, Vicki.'

She flinched away from the compassion in Nils's eyes. He had no such hope, she could tell. He thought she was snatching at straws, doing anything to avoid confronting the truth, the cold, hard facts. 'Garth should have the chance to defend himself,' she said stubbornly. 'Otherwise I'm condemning him on the basis of hearsay.'

'Newspapers don't print all that stuff just on hearsay, Vicki. Look, it's very simple. All you've got to do is get in the truck with me now, and we'll go back home. You can stay at the cabin tonight and tomorrow we'll open up your house.'

'No, Nils, I can't do that,' she said hopelessly, knowing her words would hurt him but unable to avoid it. 'I'm sorry—I just can't. Because that's not home any more, you see. Home is here—with Garth and Stephen.'

'You're a fool, Vicki!'

'Maybe I am, who knows?' she said wearily. 'I don't think it makes much difference really. Will you take me back now, please?'

He stalked across the beach and slammed the door of the truck behind him. She sat very still beside him as he backed on to the main road, tires spinning on the gravel. Up the slope to the top of the hill and there in the field was Garth's house again—their house—looking just as she had left it. It was she who was different.

Nils let her out at the bottom of the driveway. 'Do you want this?' he asked roughly, indicating the folder.

'No. I won't need it. Goodbye, Nils.'

'Vicki, I wish—oh hell, what's the use? If you need me, you know where I am.' The truck lurched back on the road and she stood watching it until it was out of sight. Only then did she begin to walk up the driveway towards the house.

CHAPTER TWELVE

GARTH was standing outside on the back step, thumbs hooked in the belt of his whipcord trousers. Vicki's footsteps dragged; she felt as though in the last hour the whole world had turned upside down. The man standing on the step had become a stranger to her, and nothing was as it should be.

As soon as she was in earshot he said, 'That was Nils, wasn't it? Why didn't he come in?'

She said the first thing that came into her head. 'He had work to do, so he had to get back.'

'I didn't know you were seeing him this afternoon.' A faint edge of suspicion in his voice.

'Neither did I—he just turned up.'

'So where did you go?'

'We went for a drive and walked on the beach for a while,' she said tonelessly.

His voice was probing. 'Did he upset you in some way?'

'What is this anyway—an inquisition?' she flared. 'Surely I have the right to a bit of private life, even though I'm married to you.'

Although obviously disconcerted by her outburst, Garth said with commendable patience, 'Vicki, I know there's something wrong. So why don't you tell me what it is?'

Over the hill trundled the bright yellow school bus and Vicki felt her knees weaken with relief. She simply wasn't ready to deal with Garth yet, and Stephen's arrival would delay the inevitable confrontation. As it happened, Stephen and the two Hunter boys got off the bus together, running up the driveway with all the frenetic energy of small boys who have been cooped up indoors on a fresh spring day. There were the inevitable after-school cookies and milk to be distributed, then Vicki allowed herself to be coerced into a rowdy game of catch out in the field;

when she finally went in the house to start supper, Garth was on the telephone in the study. Another reprieve.

He came back into the kitchen just as she was taking a pie out of the oven. Without preamble he said, 'How would you like a couple of days in Toronto?'

She straightened, carefully putting the pie on a rack to cool. 'What's going on there?' she said coolly. She could see that her tone of voice disturbed him and was suddenly, savagely, pleased.

'That was my publisher—he wants me up there for a couple of TV shows. He mentioned it earlier in the month, but what with one thing and another——' he gave her an intimate little smile which she pretended not to see, 'I'd forgotten about it. The only drawback is that we'd have to go tomorrow—but Mrs Sampson said she'd stay with Stephen if I was stuck.' He grinned boyishly. 'We could have a honeymoon after all.'

'I don't think I should go, Garth,' she said, rinsing off the potatoes and adding salt to the saucepan. 'Stephen hasn't had long enough to get used to the idea of our marriage.'

He walked over to her, removing the saucepan from her hands and holding her by the shoulders. In his eyes she read disappointment, hurt, and puzzlement. 'I don't understand—it doesn't even sound as if you want to go. I'd thought you'd be excited——'

'When I married you I became, to all intents and purposes, Stephen's mother,' she said pointedly. 'It happens to be a responsibility I take very seriously, that's all.'

His voice was clipped and purposeful. 'I'm not going to allow Stephen to come between us, Vicki. I didn't marry you to get a mother for Stephen. I married you because I wanted you for my wife—and as my wife, I want you to go to Toronto with me.'

For a brief painful moment she recognised how happy the same invitation would have made her this morning—two days alone with Garth in a busy, exciting city. Now all she could think of was how his departure would leave her blessedly alone, giving her a chance to repair some of the ravages Nils had wrought. 'Well, I'm not going,' she said, her eyes flat and unrevealing.

'Vicki, you're worrying too much about Stephen. He's used to me going away occasionally. If the two of us go together, he'll understand that we'll come back when we say.'

Of its own accord her tongue spat the words at him. 'His mother didn't come back.' She felt the shock run through his big body, saw his features tighten against the assault of a pain she had induced. Pain because Corinne, his beautiful Corinne, was dead and would never come back. . . .

His eyes impaled her and involuntarily she tried to retreat; she had never seen him look quite so dangerous before. 'You'd better explain just what you mean by that,' he said, with formidable quietness.

But before she could answer, Stephen tumbled in the back door. 'Dad, the ball fell down between some rocks and we can't reach it! Will you come and get it out?'

Trembling from a release of strain, Vicki watched the two of them leave the house, Stephen swinging wildly on his father's arm. If she could only hang on until tomorrow, she thought, then she would have two days of solitude to plan how best to cope with her devastating new knowledge . . . surely she could keep it hidden from Garth until then?

Afternoon slipped into evening. Last night Vicki had longed for the minutes to fly by until she would find herself in Garth's arms again; tonight she found herself dreading the passage of time, sensing already how intolerably difficult it would be to behave naturally.

She soon found out it was impossible. In their bedroom Garth began to undo his shirt and threw it across the chair, muscles rippling under his smooth skin. His hands reached for his belt buckle and his eyes rested on Vicki's slim figure. 'Aren't you going to take off your robe?'

His voice seemed to come from a long way away. She looked around her blankly, as though she had never been in the room before, and the rich, barbaric hues of the

Oriental rug seemed to mock her with their splendour. What was she doing here? Who was this half-naked stranger who held over her all a husband's rights?

'Vicki, are you ill? Sweetheart, tell me what's wrong.' Before she could move, he had put his arms around her and her face was against the dark, tangled hair on his chest, while under her cheek throbbed the strong, steady beat of his heart. So must he have held Corinne before his love had turned to hatred. . . .

Mindless with revulsion, she thrust him away and the graceful folds of the caftan swirled about her legs. 'Don't touch me—I can't bear it!'

She was not prepared for the swiftness and violence of his reaction. In one lithe movement he swung her over his shoulder and flung her on the bed in a tumble of silk. Then he fell beside her, his hands pinioning her arms to the bed, his face only a foot from her shocked brown eyes. 'Now,' he said grimly, 'let's hear it. You've been behaving very strangely ever since Nils left. Have you decided you're in love with him after all? If so, that's too bad. You're my wife and that's the way it's going to stay.'

Hysterical laughter bubbled up in her throat, that he could be so far from the truth. Then he was shaking her, his eyes glittering with rage. 'Answer me!'

She was released from the dead despair of the past few hours by an anger so intense that her eyes flared like gold flames. 'Yes, I'll answer you,' she said fiercely. 'And you'll wish I hadn't. Just as I wish I'd never laid eyes on you— let alone married you!'

'What the hell are you talking about?'

'Corinne,' she hissed. 'Your first wife. The mother of your son. You loved her, didn't you? I know you did— you told me so. You couldn't bear it when you thought she was going to leave you for another man. So you took the only revenge you could—you stole her son!'

Agony raked its claws across his face, and for a moment she faltered, forgetting her own pain, knowing only that she was hurting the man she loved. He dropped his head across his arm, his muttered words striking her to the heart. 'Even from the grave, she won't leave me alone. . . .'

'So it's true.' Within her any faint vestige of hope that Nils could have been mistaken died away. 'You took away her son. And before she could claim him back, she died—in your plane.' He was silent, his whole attitude one of utter defeat.

'Garth, how could you have married me, knowing all this?' she whispered, all her own pain raw in her voice.

He looked up, his face haggard. 'Don't tell me you didn't know about it? How could you have missed my darling wife's love affair with every newspaper in the country?'

Flinching from his sarcasm, she said, 'As it happens, I did miss it. I knew nothing of all this. It was Nils who told me this afternoon.'

'How upset he must have been to find out you'd already married me,' he sneered.

'Nils is my friend—naturally he was upset.'

'And you, of course, believed every word he said.'

'He said very little. He had photographs and newspaper clippings and magazine articles—after I saw all those, there wasn't much need for him to say anything.'

'And do you always believe everything you read in the newspapers?'

Frightened, but not knowing why, she said as calmly as she could, 'Garth, it was all there in black and white.'

'It's too bad you missed her on television—that was in glorious Technicolor,' he said viciously. 'It was enough to make a hardened criminal weep.'

'I can understand why you would hate her, if she wanted to live with someone else. But did you have to use Stephen as a weapon against her?' Of the whole ugly mess, this was the hardest thing to understand, the most difficult to reconcile with the Garth she knew and loved.

He sat up on the bed, the firelight casting moving shadows over the strong bones of his face and the lean contours of his chest. 'You really think I did that?' he said very quietly. 'You think I used a four-year-old child, my own son, as a pawn between myself and my wife?'

'What else can I think?' Unconsciously her hand reached out in pleading.

He struck it down with a violence that made her cry out. 'Perhaps you could have tried trusting me!' he blazed. 'You might have waited to hear my side of the story. But oh no, you had to condemn me unheard.' His brief rage burned itself out as swiftly as it had flared up. In an almost conversational tone of voice he said, 'How you must despise me now.'

There was a sheen of tears in her eyes, for he was as wrong as he could be. No matter what he had done, she had never stopped loving him, and never would. She had nothing to lose by telling him. . . . 'Garth, I——'

'No, Vicki—nothing more,' he said wearily. 'I've had all I can take for one night.' He got up and his shadow fell over the bed, dark and attenuated. 'While I'm in Toronto, we'd both better give some hard thought to where we're going from here. God knows I have no idea. In the meantime there's a couch in the study—I'll sleep there.'

She had wanted him to go, hadn't she? She had wanted to be left alone. In a rustle of turquoise and gold she got to her feet. 'Please don't go. Can't we . . .' Her voice trailed away before his wolfish smile.

'If I don't go, I shall make love to you, Vicki. Is that what you want?' His hands swooped down on her, moulding the fullness of her breasts, the curve of her waist and the rounded smoothness of her hips. His kiss was an attack, but at least it was real, it was flesh and blood after that hail of bitter, hurtful words. Briefly, mind and body warred within her. Then her arms went around him, her fingers digging into his flesh; her lips parted, wantonly inviting his invasion, and she had her answer—she wanted him, no matter what. She couldn't live without him. . . .

He flung her off so roughly that she fell back against the bed, her eyes wide with horror as she saw his ravaged face. 'What kind of woman are you?' he grated. 'You'd sleep with a man you despise? According to you I was responsible for Corinne's death. Yet you want to make love to me!'

His contempt flayed her of all pride and reticence. She straightened with a kind of desperate dignity. 'I would make love with you because you're my husband—and because I love you.'

He stepped closer and her self-control wavered before the intensity of his rage. 'You find me capable of the most despicable behaviour, yet you love me—how very touching! You'll forgive me, I'm sure, if I don't believe you. I'd have thought more of you if you'd told me you hated me!'

The words struck her like the blows of a whip and with one part of her mind she wondered if she was going to faint. She was fast reaching the end of her endurance, she knew, and the only weapon that was left to her was a bare, brutal honesty. 'It doesn't matter whether you believe me or not. It happens to be true. No matter what you've done, I love you—and I always will.'

'Get out!' Garth exploded. 'Get out of my room, and take your shoddy little ntions of love with you. Because I don't want them—do you hear me?'

His hands were curved like talons in front of him and for a terrifying instant she could feel them around her neck, squeezing the life from her. She backed around him, her face white as the sheets on the bed, her movements jerky and unco-ordinated, until she was out of the room and fleeing down the corridor to her old room. Shutting the door behind her, she wedged a chair under the handle.

Then her control broke. Terror, pain, humiliation— they washed over her with all the pent-up fury of an ocean storm, and she was tossed and thrown in a sea of bitter, tearing regret. For tonight something precious, something beautiful, had been destroyed forever. Falling face down on the bed, she began to weep. She wept until there were no tears left, and still her heart was black with sorrow and she had found no peace.

Vicki must have slept, for somehow the night passed and with daylight some of its demons fled. The soft pearly light of morning illuminated the ocean. It was calm and flat and grey and she felt a faint lightening of her spirits. The storms of the night were over. Surely the morning would be a new beginning?

She washed and dressed, using make-up to try and conceal the marks of weeping. Stephen was already in the kitchen and he seemed to notice nothing amiss. 'It's too bad Dad has to go away,' he said cheerfully, pouring himself a glass of juice. 'I'm glad you're staying home, though. Will you play ball with us after school again tomorrow?'

'Where's your father?' she asked, her throat dry.

'Getting packed. Will you?'

She stared at him blankly. 'Will I what?'

'Play ball with us after school,' he repeated impatiently.

'Yes, of course,' she murmured, every nerve tightening as she heard Garth's footsteps coming down the hall. So he had definitely decided he was going to Toronto alone, she thought, with a spurt of anger. So be it. . . . Injecting life into her voice, she said to Stephen, 'I'll call Carole today and see if the boys can have supper with us and maybe stay overnight—would you like that?'

'Yeah! That'd be great—we could play racing cars. Hey, Dad, Vicki says Andrew and Tony can stay overnight.'

'Good, that'll be company for you both,' said Garth matter-of-factly. His back to Vicki as he helped himself to cereal from the cupboard, he went on, 'My plane leaves at eleven-thirty, so I'll have to get away from here about the same time as Stephen catches the bus. I'll be back on Monday evening, about nine.'

'But that's three days!' Vicki exclaimed in dismay.

'I thought I may as well visit a few friends while I was up there,' he said coolly.

So already he was making excuses to stay away from her. Sick at heart, she put the jam and honey on the table and plugged in the toaster.

At eight-thirty Stephen raced down the driveway to catch the school bus. Alone in the kitchen, Vicki began to load the dishwasher—anything to keep busy. Rinsing off the plates, she didn't hear Garth until he spoke behind her. The plate fell from her hand and clattered into the sink.

Taking a grip on herself, she picked it up and put it in the rack. 'What did you say?'

'Leave that for a minute—I want to talk to you.'

She turned to face him. The morning light fell across her face and no amount of make-up could have hidden the violet shadows under her eyes and the tension along her jawline. 'Yes?'

He looked devastatingly attractive in a dark grey business suit, yet he was not unmarked himself: there were new lines in his face and his eyes were sunk into their sockets. 'I frightened you last night—I'm sorry.' She could think of nothing to say to this, because he *had* frightened her. 'That whole thing about Corinne——' he laboured on. 'Maybe that's a ghost I'll never lay to rest, I don't know. But I'm damned if I'm going to justify myself to you or to anyone else. If you choose to believe all that publicity—well, that's up to you.' His manner quietened. 'While I'm away, you'd better decide what you want to do next—stay or leave.'

Appalled, Vicki wondered if she was hearing him right—and knew from the granite-hard eyes that she was. 'Do you want me to leave?'

'That seems a bit irrelevant. You're going to have to make up your own mind, Vicki—I won't do it for you.'

Again she had that tragic sense of having destroyed something fragile and precious. Garth wouldn't fight for her, that was what he was saying—because she wasn't worth it? Numbly she realised he was still speaking.

'We'll talk again when I get back.'

The numbness spread through her body, paralysing her tongue. He picked up his leather suitcase and a smaller briefcase, and put his raincoat over his arm. 'If you need a car for anything, I'm sure you can borrow the Hunters'. I left the name and phone number of my hotel on the dresser in my room in case of any emergency.' He halted, something in the girl's frozen stillness penetrating his own composure. As though the words were dragged from him, he said, 'Take care of yourself, won't you?'

'You, too,' she whispered.

The slightest nod of acknowledgment and then he was striding across the room as though he could not wait to be gone. Down the stairs. Out the back door. Then the sound of his car engine, diminishing as he backed down the driveway.

Vicki ran down the hallway to his bedroom, pushing back the long nylon drapes so she could see the road, and standing statue-still until the car went out of sight down the hill. Only then did she turn back to the room. She had known happiness such as she had never known before in this room. On that bed she and Garth had kissed and touched and loved with a tenderness and intimacy she could not have imagined. And then last night that golden world of delight that they had created between them had spun off its axis and exploded into a thousand pieces, leaving a black emptiness that no one else could ever fill.

Moving without conscious thought, she neatly folded back the bedspread and slipped off her shoes. Getting into bed, she buried her face in the pillow, where there was the slightest hint of the clean masculine scent of Garth's skin. Too tired to cry, she closed her eyes and fell asleep.

CHAPTER THIRTEEN

VICKI slept until early afternoon, and it must have been what she needed, for she woke with her brain working once more and with a clear-cut sense of purpose: she was not going to run from this marriage. What she and Garth had shared together so briefly was worth fighting for, and she was going to fight.

Now, as she looked back on the attack and counter-attack of the evening before, she saw what she had been too upset to see before: Garth had not denied his complicity in involving Stephen in that dreadful triangle, but neither had he admitted it. There *must* have been extenuating circumstances. The Garth she loved would never have risked Stephen's happiness. If he had genuinely thought it was better for Stephen to be with Corinne, then he would have left him with Corinne. That he had taken his son away indicated some basic flaw in Corinne's care of him. All she, Vicki, had to do was find out what that flaw had been . . . she grinned at herself ruefully in Garth's mirror as she splashed cold water on her face. Easier said than done, no doubt about that. But at least she was thinking straight again, not reeling from shock to shock like a rag doll.

The two Hunter boys came home with Stephen and the three of them played noisily and energetically all evening, which did not stop them from giggling in their sleeping bags until well after ten o'clock. They had finally settled down when the phone rang. Vicki leaped to answer it—maybe it was Garth.

'Hi, Vicki,' Carole greeted her, 'I just wondered if you'd survived the evening.'

'Just,' Vicki responded with a laugh. 'I think they've finally fallen asleep. They'll probably be as grouchy as bears tomorrow.'

'Maybe they'll surprise you and sleep in.'

'Were I so lucky!'

Carole laughed. 'I'll tell you why I called. Phil is supposed to go to a potters' guild meeting tomorrow night, but they're having it at Shorefield and you know how long a drive that is. He was wondering if you'd mind coming over and staying with me while he's gone. He probably won't be back until quite late, so Stephen could go to bed over here.'

'I'd love to,' Vicki replied warmly, knowing it would help her pass the time until Garth got back. 'What time should I come?'

'He's leaving around three, so any time before that would be fine—he'll come and get you.'

'Why don't I keep Andrew and Tony until then? It would give you a chance to have a quiet morning.'

'Bless you! I *am* feeling tired lately. Phil was thinking he shouldn't go, but the doctor said it could be another week, and I hate for him to miss the meeting—so many of his friends will be there.'

'I'll see you tomorrow afternoon, then.'

'Lovely! 'Bye for now.'

The next day, as thoughts of Garth and Corinne and Stephen filled her mind, Vicki was not feeling quite so sure of herself. What if there had been extenuating circumstances—would Garth ever forgive her for jumping to all the wrong conclusions? And if there were not—what then? An unanswerable question.

It was a relief to be going to Carole's, for the redhead's vivacity and irreverent sense of humour would be a welcome diversion. But Carole's greeting was unexpectedly discerning. 'Come in, Vicki—goodness, you look dreadful!'

'Carole——' Philip protested. 'Tact is *not* your middle name.'

'Well, she does look dreadful,' Carole defended herself. 'You must be missing Garth, are you?'

'Yes, I am,' Vicki admitted, her face suddenly pinched. 'A lot.'

'Oh, dear—any other time but this and we could have kept Stephen for you, so you could have gone to Toronto with Garth. Maybe Mrs Sampson would have stayed with Stephen—we sometimes get her overnight.'

'We thought of that,' Vicki said smoothly. 'But it was all a bit rushed and there really wasn't time to make arrangements. Let's hope another time I'll be able to go,' she finished, sending up a quick prayer that there would be another time.

Philip left shortly afterwards and the two women settled down in the living room with their tea. It seemed to get dark earlier than usual, and as Vicki helped Carole with supper preparations she said apprehensively, 'Look at those black clouds. And the wind is coming up. I didn't hear a weather forecast today, did you?'

'No,' Carole admitted. 'I hope Philip will have the sense to stay at Shorefield if we should have bad weather.'

'But it would only be rain——'

'This road can get pretty treacherous in a rainstorm— muddy and slippery. Oh well, maybe it won't amount to anything.' Carole reached across the counter for the paring knife and suddenly stopped midway, pressing her hand to her side.

'Carole! Are you all right?'

'Mmm . . .' said Carole shakily, sitting down rather heavily on the nearest chair. 'Just a twinge, I guess.'

At that very moment the first raindrops spattered across the windowpanes. Vicki picked up the knife herself to finish peeling the carrots, wondering uneasily what she would do if Carole went into labour now, with both Philip and Garth away, the three boys to be looked after, and a storm on the way. Chiding herself almost immediately for being overly apprehensive, she put the vegetables on to cook and checked the roast, giving Carole a quick side-ways glance as she did so.

Carole's hand was still pressed to her side, her expression turned inward upon itself. Not knowing what else to do, Vicki continued with the supper preparations, al-though she could not help feeling disquieted by the in-

creasing salvos of rain against the house and the sudden
wind-squalls that rattled the windows. When they
gathered around the table, Carole ate very little of the
meal, although Vicki managed to keep the boys' attention
so that they noticed nothing amiss. After they had disappeared to watch a favourite television show, Carole said
quietly, 'I think I'll have to go to the hospital, Vicki—I
don't think this is a false alarm. Will you make some
phone calls for me, please? Call Dr Donkin first—his
number's on the front page of the phone book. Then call
Mrs Sampson and see if she'll stay with the boys—I don't
want to have to take them out on a night like this. If she
can come, you'll have to go and get her. The truck's in
the garage, and the keys are in my handbag. I'll call
Philip after I've seen Dr Donkin.'

Carole's own calmness had a steadying effect on Vicki
and she quickly went to the phone. The doctor advised
bringing Mrs Hunter in immediately; and yes, Mrs
Sampson would be glad to look after the boys. Vicki
pulled on a jacket and took the keys. 'I'll be back in
twenty minutes, Carole. You'll be all right?'

There were lines of strain around the vivid green eyes.
'Yes—drive carefully.'

Vicki went out of the back door into the blackness of
the night. The wind buffeted her so strongly that she staggered; she pulled her coat around her to protect herself
from the driving rain. Once in the shelter of the garage,
she was glad to find that the truck was similar to Nils's;
she backed it out without mishap and turned on to the
road. Mrs Sampson lived only three miles away, her house
being the last one before the road turned into a narrow
track between the trees, but because of the blinding rain
Vicki had to drive very slowly. As she drew up by the
house, its lights glimmering through the rain, Mrs
Sampson's stout figure scurried down the path, head bent
against the wind, and Vicki leaned across to unlock the
door.

'What an awful night, dear! No night for a baby to be
born, is it, but then they never do choose the most con-

venient times.' Mrs Sampson had had six children of her
own, Vicki knew, so presumably knew what she was talking about. The older woman kept up a placid monologue,
requiring Vicki to only occasionally nod or shake her
head, until they arrived at Carole's; once inside, she took
over with a calm authority that was very comforting, and
in no time Carole had been helped into the front seat and
Vicki was ready to leave again, Mrs Sampson's,
'Don't worry about a thing, dear,' still echoing in her
ears.

However, once on the road to the Bay, there was plenty
for Vicki to worry about. The windshield wipers made
little impression on the sheets of rain and it took every
ounce of Vicki's concentration to see the road ahead.
Water was running in streams over the gravel surface,
and more than once the tires skidded as they sought for
traction. She soon discovered that the shoulders of the
road were far too soft for safety, so she steered straight
down the middle, knowing it was very unlikely she would
meet anyone else, worrying nevertheless what she would
do if she did. From the corner of her eye she caught
glimpses of the wind-tossed boughs of the spruce trees;
what with the rain and the metallic rattling of the truck
and the roaring of the wind, the noise was deafening.

At the crest of the hill Vicki slowed down momentarily,
sparing Carole a quick glance. 'How are you doing?'

Carole grimaced. 'The contractions are about ten
minutes apart. How much longer do you think we'll be?'

'Half an hour?' she hazarded, creeping down the slope
in low gear.

'Do you mind if I talk?' Carole asked abruptly. 'It helps
keep my mind off things.'

'Go ahead,' said Vicki, raising her voice in order to be
heard. 'I wonder if the weather's like this where Philip
is?'

'Probably—I wish I'd phoned him from the house. He
could have been on his way by now.'

'Was he with you when the boys were born?'

'Oh yes, it's a time when I really need him. You'll

know what I mean when you and Garth have your first baby.'

Vicki frowned unconsciously, carefully edging the truck over a culvert, its metal piping exposed where the fill had been washed away by the rain. The mere thought of carrying Garth's child filled her with such a bittersweet emotion that she could not bring herself to reply. She longed for it . . . and equally she feared it would never occur.

'You and Garth do want children, don't you?' As Vicki winced, Carole added, 'Oh dear, have I said something I shouldn't? I'm always doing that.'

'No, it's all right, it's just that. . . .' Her voice trailed away.

'I'm sorry—it's none of my business.'

Carole was too good a friend to be fobbed off like that. 'Garth and I had an awful argument the night before he went away. I don't know what's going to happen when he comes back.' Vicki's hands gripped the steering wheel as it shuddered, the truck rocking on its wheel base from the force of the gale.

'I wondered if something like that had happened,' Carole yelled back, and it suddenly struck Vicki what an incongruous conversation this was at such a time and in such a place. But then Carole's fingers fastened on the dash and her face contorted with pain, and Vicki knew she would talk about anything under the sun if it would help. Finally Carole raised her head again and sat back in the seat. 'Why were you arguing? Phil and I nearly got divorced at one point on our honeymoon!'

Amazingly Vicki found she could laugh. 'It was about Corinne—his first wife,' she admitted, and there was a strange relief in bringing it out into the open.

'Good heavens! She's not worth arguing about.'

'What do you mean? You didn't even know her.'

'Oh yes, we did,' Carole said warmly. 'Didn't I ever tell you that we knew them both years ago, when Phil and I were still living in Toronto? Corinne was a bitch if ever there was one.'

'You're joking—she was gorgeous.'

'Handsome is as handsome does,' Carole said tritely. 'Corinne Travis was the most selfish, spiteful, greedy, brazen hussy I've ever met.'

'But, Carole——'

'No buts. You didn't know her—we did.' She peered out of the side window. 'We're almost at the Bay, aren't we?'

'Yes. The hospital's a couple of miles beyond that, isn't it?'

'Right. She was a dreadful mother, too, neglecting poor Stephen from the day he was born. She neglected Garth as well, of course, except that after a while I think he was delighted to be left alone. She had no time for either of them. She was always gadding about from film to film, and from lover to lover——'

'She was unfaithful to him more than once?'

'Hasn't he told you any of this?' Carole demanded incredulously.

'No. It was almost as though she'd never existed.'

'Good lord! Although I can hardly blame him for wanting to forget her—she made his life a hell on earth. Her first lover—with whom she went away when Stephen was two months old—happened to be Garth's best friend. That was typical of Corinne.'

They were driving through the scattered houses of the Bay now, and visibility was noticeably better. 'I can't believe it,' Vicki muttered. 'I saw photographs of her taken before the court case. She looked so tragic, so incredibly beautiful.'

'I never said she wasn't a good actress,' Carole responded crisply. 'She milked that situation for all it was worth, and the sad thing is that every housewife in the country thought Corinne was the wronged wife and the bereaved mother. Do you know why she wanted Stephen?'

'I thought it was because she loved him.'

'You couldn't be farther from the truth. . . .' Again there was that aching pause as Carole's head bent, her hands grabbing the dashboard. When she began again her voice was thinner and Vicki had to strain to catch the words. 'She was having an affair with a famous director, Stanislaus Protsky. He was very much a family man—a widower devoted to his children. So all of a sudden Corinne had to change her image. She took Stephen to her apartment when Garth was away and started such a blaze of publicity that Garth had no choice—he had to take her to court for custody of the son he had cared for ever since he was born.'

In a swift flashback Vicki saw in front of her eyes the photographs of Garth leaving the restaurant, and later at Corinne's funeral—bitter, unhappy, beleaguered on every side. 'He looked after Stephen all along,' she repeated slowly, and knew it had to be the truth.

'Well, of course. To anyone who knew Garth, it was obvious where Stephen belonged. But by a very skilful manipulation of the media and of public opinion, Corinne turned him into a monster. Oh, it still makes me furious when I think about it!'

Vicki had longed for extenuating circumstances, and now she had them—beyond a doubt, impossible to dispute. 'Oh, Carole,' she moaned, 'I was as bad as the rest of them, because I believed Corinne's story as well. I couldn't understand how he could take Stephen from his mother's arms. I even accused him of using Stephen as a pawn . . . no wonder he was so furious!'

'If he hadn't told you anything, I don't see how he could blame you for jumping to all the wrong conclusions,' Carole said briskly.

'I should have trusted him.'

'Corinne could make you believe black was white,' was the unequivocal reply. 'So stop berating yourself. Apologise to Garth, tell him you love him—and everything will be all right, you'll see.'

Vicki frowned. She had done just that, and everything had not been all right. It had been as wrong as it could be . . . but there was no time to tell Carole that, for through the squalls of rain she saw the illuminated blue and white hospital sign, and on the side of the hill its

well-lit, comfortingly solid bulk. 'We made it,' she said
ith relief, driving over to the emergency entrance. 'Stay
put for a minute.' Jumping down from the truck, she ran
inside to get Carole a wheelchair.

Within minutes the hospital's swift and efficient routine
had taken over. Before Carole was wheeled away, she said
to Vicki, 'Don't feel you have to stay, I expect you're
anxious to get back to the boys. I spoke to Phil and he's
leaving now, so I'll be okay.' Her eyes for once deadly
serious, she said, 'Vicki, thanks—and remember my
advice. I don't have to tell you that Garth can be pretty
formidable—but just remember that Corinne hurt him
about as badly as a woman could, and make allowances,
hmm?'

Vicki bent and kissed Carole's pale cheek. 'I'll remember,' she promised. 'And I'll be waiting to hear about
the baby.'

Carole tossed her red curls. 'After all this, it had better
be a girl!'

So there was a smile on Vicki's lips as she walked along
the shiningly clean corridors with their unmistakable hospital odour of disinfectant and floor wax and starched
linen. However, at the front door the tumult of wind and
rain made her pause. In one way she dreaded the drive
back to Seal Cove through the storm, particularly now
that she would be alone. But something in her wanted to
be home again, even though Garth wasn't due back for
two more days. Maybe he would phone. Or she could
phone him—yes, that was what she would do. It was too
important to their future to delay a reconciliation any
longer. Decisively she pushed open the door and ran for
the truck.

She made fair progress until she reached the other side
of the Bay. But there both weather and road conditions
worsened appreciably and she had to slow the vehicle to a
crawl, her hands tense on the wheel, her eyes straining
into the darkness ahead of her. The rear of the truck
slewed all over the road under the onslaught of the wind,
and twice the wheels almost mired down in the mud. Her

heart in her mouth, she kept going, accelerating up the hills, inching down them, nerve-rackingly conscious of the sheer drop-off on her right where the cliff face fell to the sea. In the occasional lull of the gale, she could hear the ocean's hungry roar as the waves dashed themselves on to the jagged rocks so far below.

Her arms and wrists were aching from the strain of wrestling with the wheel, just as her eyes ached from penetrating the blur of rain. But she knew she was getting close to home now—only another two or three miles to go. She pushed down on the gas pedal, the tires throwing back a shower of pebbles and dirt as she topped a rise.

The tree that lay across the road was invisible to her until she was almost on top of it. She gasped with fear, her foot jamming on the brake. The truck veered wildly and for a horrifying moment she thought she was going to go over the cliff. But then the back end slammed against the tree trunk and the truck ricocheted the other way, toppling into the ditch. Her head struck the door. Even then she had the presence of mind to turn off the ignition key before she slumped, dazed and trembling, against the seat.

It could have been five minutes, it could have been thirty, before Vicki dragged herself upright, feeling sick and shaken and very cold. Rain beat on the roof. The windshield had shattered and through the cracks water dripped monotonously to the floor. There was a strong smell of gasoline, and it was this that galvanised hr into action. She had to get out of here. Awkwardly zipping up her jacket, she pulled the hood over her head, and with some confused idea of theft, shoved her handbag part way under the seat. The door on her side had jammed. Wincing from a pain in her shoulder, she edged across to the other side and against the force of the wind pushed the door open and scrambled to the ground. If only she had a flashlight ... as an afterthought, she hurriedly reached into the truck again and pulled the hazard button, so that the rear lights began to flash on and off; there did not seem to be anything else she could do to warn any other travellers on the road.

Clenching her teeth to stop them chattering, she looked around her in the intermittent red light. The tree was a huge spruce, its roots clogged with red mud; she could see the marks it had gouged in the bank when it had fallen across the road. It was far too heavy to be moved by one person. She clambered over it with some difficulty, discovering several new aches and pains in her body as she did so. Still, she considered herself lucky, for apart from bruising and a certain lightheadedness, she had escaped without injury.

Beyond the tree the road disappeared into the wind-torn darkness. Mentally bracing herself, she shoved her hands into her pockets and began trudging along it, her footing uncertain until her eyes adjusted to the darkness. Even then she still slithered and slipped her way down the hill and within five minutes she was soaked to the skin, wet hair plastered to her face and water trickling down into her rubber boots. She tried to walk faster to keep warm, but her knees had started shaking again and all she could manage was a kind of shuffling gait. Twice she tripped and fell, the second time crashing face down on to the road, knocking the breath from her lungs and scraping her face on the loose gravel. She struggled upright, fighting back dizziness. It couldn't be much far-ther—a mile? a mile and a half? She was so tired. . . . All she wanted to do was find a dry place out of the rain and fall asleep until morning. Without having consciously made a decision she struggled up the bank on her hands and knees and huddled under the spreading boughs of a spruce, resting her aching head on her knees. Reality drifted away into a confused nightmare of the wind's fin-gers plucking at her sodden clothes, its voice mingled with the constant mutter and growl of the sea. . . .

There was another voice, and it was calling her name. She fought her way back to consciousness, totally dis-orientated. Where was she? What was she doing here? Carole—what had happened to Carole? Panic-stricken, she tried to stand up and heard again, tossed on the wind, the sound of her name. 'Vicki . . . Vicki!' She must get up. Garth was looking for her.

Primitive terror struck her to the heart so that she clung to the branches for support. It couldn't be Garth—Garth was in Toronto. So whose voice was calling her from the darkness? Luring her out of her shelter into the open . . . waiting for her. . . .

Her heart pumping with fear, she edged forward to peer down into the road and her foot loosened a miniature rockslide over the bank. A beam of yellow light swung round out of the blackness and transfixed her, all white face and huge eyes.

'Vicki!' the same voice cried, hoarse with emotion. 'Sweetheart—are you all right?' Behind the flashlight she could see only an anonymous black bulk.

'Garth?' she whispered.

The beam lowered as the man scaled the bank and then his arms were around her, holding her as if he would never let her go. 'I thought I'd never find you,' he muttered into her ear. 'Why were you driving Philip's truck—was it because of Carole?'

'I had to take her to the hospital. Philip wasn't home. I didn't see the tree until it was too late.'

'If you hadn't left the truck lights on, I might not have either.'

His arms were firm and sure, and she was safe again. 'It's Monday you're coming home,' she murmured foolishly.

'I came early. Look, we'd better get home before we start on any explanations. You're soaked, love.'

That tiny word disarmed her as nothing else could have. 'I'm all right,' she said. 'Now that you're here.'

As though he couldn't prevent himself, Garth kissed her once, hard. His arms around her, he helped her back to the road. Sheltered by his body and with the flashlight showing the way, Vicki managed to keep up a fair pace and slowly warmth began to seep back into her limbs. They climbed the final hill and a few minutes later came to their own driveway. Up the back steps and then Garth was unlocking the door and ushering her inside. The storm's cacophony was hushed as he closed the door behind him. It was warm and dry, and she was safe. She sank into the nearest chair.

Garth flipped on the light. 'What happened to your face?' he demanded.

She fingered her dirty cheek, suppressing a shudder of recollection. 'I fell and scraped it.'

He pulled off his boots and his black rain slicker. Underneath, incongruously enough, he was wearing the same dark business suit he had had on when he left. 'Just let me change these trousers—I'll be right back,' he said.

Within minutes he returned, wearing soft cords and a crew-necked sweater. He tugged off her jacket and boots and then picked her up as easily as if she were Stephen, carrying her down to their bedroom.

As he began stripping off her wet clothes, he asked matter-of-factly, 'Where's Stephen? Is there anyone I should be phoning?'

'The hospital, to see how Carole is. And Mrs Sampson—she's over at the Hunters' with the three boys.'

'Okay—I'll do that while you're having a shower. Off you go.'

In the bathroom she turned on the taps and the hot water began to envelop her in steam. Garth would look after everything, she knew, and she was content to have it so. All that mattered was that he had come back to her.

When she emerged, her body wrapped in a fluffy white towel, another towel around her hair turban-fashion, Garth was waiting for her, a wide smile on his face. 'Phil arrived at the hospital just in time to greet the arrival of his new daughter—and Carole's fine. So I passed the good news on to Mrs Sampson. She'll stay there until the road's cleared and we can get the car through.'

'That's wonderful news—Carole must be on top of the world!' she exclaimed. 'They both so wanted a daughter.'

The fire was throwing a glorious heat and she sank down on her knees, holding out her hands, through her pleasure suddenly very conscious of the fact that she and

Garth were alone in the house.

Garth began to rub her hair dry, brushing it until it crackled and shone with a fire of its own. Then he sat close beside her on the sheepskin rug, and her heart began to beat a little faster. 'So that's everyone else looked after,' he said quietly. 'Which leaves the two of us to talk about.' His eyes darkened as they drank in the beauty of her heart-shaped face with its grave smile and petal-smooth skin. As though compelled by a force stronger than himself, he bent forward and his lips brushed hers with an exquisite gentleness.

Vicki's whole body sprang into life and suddenly his hands were roving her shoulders and the towel had slipped to her waist and he was groaning her name. She felt herself being lifted to her feet. The towel was slipping still further and nothing mattered in the world but the two of them.

Straining her to his body, Garth said thickly, 'We don't need to talk about *this*, do we, Vicki?'

She ran her hands under his shirt, her eyes golden with happiness and clear with an absolute trust in the rightness of what they were doing. Her answer was to put her arms around his neck, lifting her face for his kiss.

He took her in an impassioned silence, mouth and hands and body mutely expressing his need of her, his homage to her beauty, his hunger. She gave him back pleasure for pleasure, until the silence was broken by the harshness of his breathing, her whimpers of delight. Together they climbed to unbearable heights and then as one toppled over the edge, to lie spent and panting, naked limbs tangled in the sheets.

Finally, Garth raised himself on one elbow. 'Vicki,' he said very seriously, 'about the other night——'

She had known this must come. Deliberately she cupped his face in her hands, staring straight into the troubled grey of his eyes. 'Please will you forgive me, Garth?' she whispered. When he would have spoken she checked him with a little shake of her head. 'I should have known you could never have done all those dreadful things the newspapers—and Corinne—accused you of.

I'm sorry I let myself believe them, even for a minute. I suppose it was the shock of coming across it all at once.'

'And that's my fault,' he said heavily. 'I should have told you the whole story before we married. My only excuse is that I hated the thought of dragging it all up again.'

'I can understand that,' she said softly. 'Why do you think I never told you the truth about Barry and me, until I absolutely had to?'

'We both had secrets from each other, didn't we?'

'But not any more. Carole told me the truth about Corinne and Stephen. It must have been a terrible time for you.'

'I did feel very much alone against the world,' he said with an attempted lightness that did not quite succeed. 'The other thing I'm sorry for is my behaviour before I went away—instead of storming off to Toronto I should have stayed home and told you the whole story then. I did a lot of thinking in Toronto. I had to come home early—to tell you I was sorry.'

'We both made mistakes,' she said very quietly.

'Perhaps that's a part of a real marriage,' he said with a humility that touched her to the heart. 'Making mistakes. Then talking about them, as we are now, and mending the hurt, so that we grow closer in the process.'

There was pink in her cheeks and her eyes were soft as velvet. Briefly she rested her forehead on his bare shoulder, feeling his arms come around here, gently caressing her back. 'We have grown closer,' she said, her voice bell-like with happiness.

Garth lifted her head, his fingers twined in her hair. 'There's one other thing you said that night that I haven't been able to get off my mind.'

Her eyes clouded. 'I said a lot of things I shouldn't have.'

'Oh, I think this needed to be said. You said you loved me—do you remember that?' Her heightened colour was all the answer he needed. 'Did you mean it, Vicki?'

Not for anything would she lie to him. She raised her

chin proudly. 'Yes, I meant it. I do love you. But, Garth, I can understand that after Corinne you might find it impossible to love anyone else.'

He was smiling at her, a smile that made her lips tremble and her eyes shine. 'Now, when I look back, I'm no longer so sure I ever did love her. Although I thought I did at the time. The feelings I had for her don't seem to bear much relationship to the feelings I have for you. It's you I love, Vicki—and you I will love until the day I die.'

'Oh, Garth. . . .' The tears that shone on her lashes were tears of sheer happiness and she knew there was no need to explain that to him. 'I thought you still loved Corinne. I certainly never thought you loved me—that was why I couldn't understand why you wanted to marry me.'

'I wanted to marry you the first moment I saw you, standing in the doorway with an axe in your hand. As brave and beautiful as a lioness protecting her cub—only the cub was mine. I knew I had to make you mine as well. I can't explain it, Vicki. I just knew that we belonged together, and I couldn't rest until we were married. Then when we did get married, we nearly threw it all away.'

Fierce as a lioness she said, 'We won't do that again.'

'No, I don't think we will.' His hands slid from her shoulders to cup her breasts and between them the diamond he had given her sparkled and flashed. 'Happy?'

Her whole body sang to his touch. Unashamedly she let him see her pleasure. 'Happier than I ever thought I could be.'

'Love me?'

Her voice trembled. 'So much. . . .'

There was a ghost of a remembered pain in his voice. 'And all along I thought you were marrying me for Stephen's sake.'

'I love Stephen, too. But he isn't the reason I married you.' Her eyes searched his face anxiously. 'You do believe me, don't you?'

'Yes, I believe you.' His eyes lingered over the length of her body, possessive and sure. 'Do you remember once—and it seems a very long time ago—I told you there would be no spring for you?'

'Yes, I remember that. I was afraid you were right, too.'

'I was wrong, Vicki.' He kissed her again. 'For both of us, summer is just beginning.'

Harlequin Plus

A WORD ABOUT THE AUTHOR

Born in England, Sandra Field today makes her home in Nova Scotia, Canada. Converts, she says, are usually fanatical in their new beliefs, and Sandra is strongly attached to the Maritimes, with its sometimes inhospitable climate but breathtakingly beautiful scenery.

She has lived in all three of Canada's Maritime provinces, but it was during her stay on tiny Prince Edward Island, where the beaches are legendary but the winters long, that she decided to write a book. The local library provided her with a guide for aspiring authors, and she followed the instructions to a "t."

It was no simple job, she recalls now. In fact, a major crisis occurred when she ran out of plot several thousand words short of the mark! But a good friend coaxed her into completing the manuscript for the simple reason that she wanted to read it. The book was *To Trust My Love* (Romance #1870), published in 1975.

Her many interests, which she likes to weave into her stories, include birdwatching, studying wild flowers and participating in such winter activities as snowshoeing and cross-country skiing. She particularly enjoys classical music, especially that of the Romantic period.

Readers all over the country say Harlequin is the best!

"You're #1."

A.H.*, Hattiesburg, Missouri

"Harlequin is the best in romantic reading."

K.G., Philadelphia, Pennsylvania

"I find Harlequins are the only stories on the market that give me a satisfying romance, with sufficient depth without being maudlin."

C.S., Bangor, Maine

"Keep them coming! They are still the best books."

R.W., Jersey City, New Jersey

*Names available on request.

FREE!
Romance Treasury

**A beautifully bound,
value-packed,
three-in-one
volume of romance!**

Romance Treasury

An exciting opportunity to collect treasured
works of romance! Almost 600 pages of exciting
romance reading in each beautifully bound
hardcover volume!

You may cancel your subscription whenever you wish!
You don't have to buy any minimum number of
volumes. Whenever you decide to stop your
subscription just drop us a line and we'll cancel all
further shipments.